NIGHT OF THE FIFTH MOON

anna ciddor

ALLEN&UNWIN

This project has been assisted by the Australian Government through the Australia Council, its arts funding and advisory body.

First published in 2007

Allen & Unwin
83 Alexander St
Crows Nest NSW 2065
Australia
Phone: (61 2) 8425 0100
Fax: (61 2) 9906 2218
Email: info@allenandunwin.com
Web: www.allenandunwin.com

National Library of Australia
Cataloguing-in-Publication entry:

Ciddor, Anna.
Night of the fifth moon.
ISBN 9781741148145 (pbk).
1. Druids and druidism – Juvenile fiction. I. Title.
A823.3

Cover and text design by Tabitha King
Typefaces include First Order from Iconian Fonts at
http://www.iconian.com/
Typeset by Midland Typesetters, Australia
Printed by McPherson's Printing Group

10 9 8 7 6 5 4 3 2 1

Teachers' notes available from www.allenandunwin.com

CONTENTS

only a true druid can read this message

The Omen

The sun was dying in the sky as Faelán the Druid, swathed in a long cloak of blue-green feathers, glided towards the fire. His eyes, like clear pools, glinted with tiny reflected images of the flames, and his hair, the colour of moonbeams, hung in long, twisting locks below his shoulders.

'Maybe he'll let us join in today,' whispered Ket.

'And maybe the trees'll lay eggs,' muttered Bran.

'He's got to let us join in *some* time!'

Every day Ket raced around doing all the tasks that Faelán bid him. He picked nettles till his arms stung with pain from the pricking of the thorns. He clambered up the highest trees and crawled on swaying, brittle branches to fetch feathers from the birds' nests for the druid's cloaks. He stood for hours in freezing mountain streams trapping fish with his bare hands, while his legs turned to ice and leeches sucked his blood.

And every day he watched for a sign from the druid. For he knew that one day the druid would make him an assistant – an anruth. One day he would learn the druid's secrets and take part in the mystic ceremonies. One day . . .

Faelán lifted his branch of golden bells, and Ket bent eagerly forward. But, as usual, the druid turned his back on the group of fosterlings.

'It's not fair,' pouted Riona.

Ket gulped back a sigh and watched with envy as the four anruth began to circle the fire, their long grey robes almost touching the flames.

'Spirit of the Moon
Arise from darkness
Spirit of the Moon
Return and guide us,'

they chanted.

Slowly, the daylight seeped away, and there, hovering near the horizon, was the tiny, fragile crescent of a new moon.

The anruth beamed with pride, then Goll, the tallest, turned and beckoned to the fosterlings. As the six of them scurried across the clearing, Goll pressed a finger to his lips. Faelán still stood with his head tilted back, searching for signs.

With muffled whispers, the fosterlings slipped into their places, and waited. A gust of wind brought an icy spatter of rain and Ket gritted his teeth. It would be another freezing, miserable night, and there was nothing to sleep on but wet leaves and hard ground.

Rain sizzled into the fire, and the brew of wild grass and badger bones bubbled and steamed.

'I'm *starving*,' hissed Nath-í.

Ket nodded agreement.

'I could go for days without food if I had to,' asserted Lorccán in a loud whisper.

Bran let out a snort.

'Ssh!' Nessa shook her head, and the little gold balls at the ends of all her braids clicked and jingled. Riona stifled a giggle.

The druid lowered his gaze, and the firelight illumined his thin, furrowed face.

'Master Faelán,' called Goll, 'what shall this day be good for?'

As he spoke, there was a squawk from a nearby tree. Everyone turned in surprise. At such an hour the birds should be asleep. Into the astonished silence flapped the shadowy shape of a raven. It flew so close, Ket could feel the wind of its passing. He stared at the black, glossy wings and knew this was an omen.

Faelán's cloak shimmered in the firelight as he

followed its flight. There was no sound but the beating of wings till the raven passed from view, then, slowly and solemnly, the druid faced the inquiring eyes. His words cut into the silence.

'This,' he announced, 'is the day for a new beginning.' His gaze swept the circle, and came to rest on the group of fosterlings.

'It's us!' Nessa gripped Ket's arm. 'It's a portent for us!'

Faelán nodded. 'Five times have the harvests been sown and reaped while you fosterlings coveted the bells and robes of the anruth. Five times have the trees budded and shed while I watched for the auspicious hour. Now, at last, the sign has come. However . . .' He raised a warning finger. 'It is not as you expect. Only one of you will become an anruth.'

The fosterlings gasped and stared at each other in dismay.

'But . . . that means only one of us can learn to be a druid!' said Nessa.

'Which one?' asked Riona.

Lorccán thrust back his shoulders and looked at the druid with bright, expectant eyes.

Faelán tugged the end of his long beard. 'I have not yet decided.'

Nath-í's long, gangly body seemed to collapse. 'It won't be me,' he mumbled.

Ket couldn't speak. His stomach was squeezed into a tight, nervous ball.

'From now until the next new moon,' Faelán went on, 'I will teach you some of the Knowledge. I will set tasks and watch you. When the dark nights return, you will know your time of judgement is nigh. And when we gather here again to welcome the rising of the next new moon, one of you will be sent away. So we will continue from new moon to new moon, till only two of you remain. Then, on the night of the fifth moon . . .'

The druid drew a smooth rod of birchwood from his girdle. He heated the point of a dagger in the fire and began to burn something in the wood. Ket stared at the blackened strokes appearing on the smooth surface. He knew they were a message written in ogham, the secret code of the druids, but he had no idea what they said.

The druid faced away from the fire and held the rod towards the Sacred Yew. 'Spirit of the Tree, I entrust this rod into your keeping,' Faelán intoned.

Stooping under the dense, dark canopy of branches, he jammed the birchwood upright between its roots. Kneeling half in shadow, half in firelight, he turned to speak.

'Writing is a skill that is sacred and secret to the druids, to help us remember our great store of knowledge.' He rested his hand on the rod. 'When only two of you remain, the one true anruth will succeed in reading this. It shall remain here till the chosen one is found.'

Ket stared in anguish at the black, meaningless strokes. How was he supposed to work it out?

The druid smiled as he rose to his feet. 'Keep your eyes and your ears open. You will find clues to guide you,' he said.

The Battle

That night, when the excited whispers of the other fosterlings had given way to slow, steady breathing, Ket lay tense and wakeful, his mind alive with images. He was living again the day he had first seen the druid, the day of the battle more than five years before . . .

The door was crashing open and the flames of the firepit roared high as Bríd burst into the room, the wind rushing in behind her.

'Quick! Hide!'

The women looked up, startled, from their cooking and spinning; the children stopped their squabbling to stare.

'The Niall clan's . . . attacking us!' Bríd gasped out, eyes wide with fear, one hand clutching her long skirt.

Then everyone leapt to their feet. Stools clattered, spindles tumbled and children squealed. They charged across the room for the trapdoor, long skirts and braids tangling together as they all tried to squeeze down the hole at once.

'Ow, that's my hair!'

'Don't push!'

'Help, the ladder's wobbling!'

They disappeared down the trapdoor, and Ket heard his mother's shrill wail from deep inside the earth, *'Ket, where's Ket?'*

But Ket crouched where he was.

'I don't belong with the babies,' he growled. 'I'm nearly seven. I should be out with the men. Fighting!'

The cries and hurrying footsteps grew muffled, and Ket was left alone, staring around him. Though his father was the chieftain of the tuath, Ket shared a home, as everyone did, with uncles and aunts, cousins and foster cousins. Twenty people ate, slept and lived in that one round room, and it was always brimming with people and noise. But now it was eerily empty.

Ket's feet rustled on the rush-strewn floor as he padded to the door and peeked out.

The yard of the ringfort was deserted, the only movement a fluttering leaf caught between the cobbles, but in the fields beyond the walls there were shouts and the blare of trumpets.

Ket scuttled across the empty yard in his bare feet, scrambled up the steps to the top of the rampart, and stretched up to peer through the spiky barrier of blackthorn. He saw Niall warriors, ferocious in war paint, marching up the hill, beating drums and blowing trumpets. From all the surrounding ringforts, men of the Cormac clan raced to meet them, hurdling over their low stone fences, yelling in fury. With a thrill of pride, Ket watched his father Ossian leap on his pony and gallop through a field of barley, cleaving the sea of yellow, his red chieftain's cloak billowing out behind him.

'Victory for the Cormacs!' Ossian the Chieftain yelled.

The invaders drew to a halt, their bare chests gleaming with sweat, arms and necks glittering with gold. They had whitened hair drawn high up on their heads and eyes ringed in black paint, lurid and glaring.

'You weakly milk-fed slop pots,' they taunted. 'We'll beat you. We'll trample you into the mud!'

One of them lifted a trumpet shaped like a boar's head. When he blew it, the hinged wooden tongue made a rude, ululating bray.

'We don't fear you, you ugly, rat-faced runts!' Skidding to a halt, Uncle Ailbe flung a stone at the attackers.

There was the flash of a spear, and Ket watched in horror as Uncle Ailbe keeled over, clutching a shoulder.

Then all the Cormacs roared, and barged forward with makeshift weapons of spades, reaping hooks and stones.

Ket let out a scream as his foster brother Eo fell to the ground, to vanish beneath the trampling feet. Ket thrust a fist in his mouth, and watched the bodies hurl together, blades flashing, voices screaming. Uncle Ailbe was on his feet again, hurtling like a bull at one of the Niall clan, locking chest to chest with him, muscles straining. Ket saw the gleam of a blade in the attacker's fist. As they struggled to and fro, Ket bit so hard on his knuckles he could taste the salt-taste of blood.

A horse-drawn chariot came rattling across the plain, sunlight flashing off the metal plates of armour on the chests of the horses. Ket saw his father wheel around on his pony, and Eo stagger to his feet. When the chariot plunged into the crowd, the rider waving and shouting, the painted warriors tried to surge forward, but the Cormacs roared their defiance.

Ossian's pony reared and lunged. Uncle Ailbe

wrenched the dagger from his opponent's grasp, and sent the man stumbling backwards in terror.

'Get him, Uncle!' Ket yelled.

But just when the tide of battle was turning, just when the men of the Cormac clan were beating the invaders back, a group of boys and girls dressed in long grey robes appeared at the edge of the forest. The little Ket watched, astonished, as the noises of battle stopped in mid cry, and the warriors froze with their sword arms in the air.

A tall figure materialised from the trees and glided majestically forward. His full-length robe was the colour of shadows, and his iridescent cloak of blue-green feathers flowed from his shoulders like a waterfall. He came to a halt, standing straight as a young champion, though he already had the grizzled hair and beard of an old man. The only sound was the creak of wicker from the chariot. That was Ket's first sight of Faelán, the druid of the forest.

The tall stranger raised an arm and pointed at Ossian.

'Surrender!' he commanded.

The anruth rang their silver bells, filling the air with the sound of tinkling.

'The druid speaks!' they cried.

Then Faelán hunched his shoulders so that the feathers of his cloak rose in a crest behind his neck.

With arm outstretched, he lifted one leg from the ground and poised there, like a giant crane.

He screwed up his face so that all his power seemed to radiate from his pointed finger and one glaring eye as words poured from his tongue.

'Surrender, Ossian o Cormac.
No chief are you who brings a blight upon his people
No chief are you whose trees bear no fruit
No chief are you whose corn droops on the stalk
No chief are you whose cows give no milk.'

The crowd booed at Ossian. Even the people from his own clan were hissing and booing at their chieftain. The druid had bent them to his will, wiping away their memories of the bulging sacks of grain, the casks of butter laid in the cool of the bog, the storage pits filled with apples and plums . . .

'It's not true! Don't listen!' shrilled Ket, but his voice was drowned out by the jeering.

He watched in helpless amazement. The effect of the druid's words was inexorable as the flood of a tide.

Faelán's gaze seared the crowd, quelling their cries.

'Surrender, Ossian o Cormac
Your prosperity is at an end
You are no longer chieftain
Ossian, grandson of Cormac.
Surrender!'

With the druid's words rising to a crescendo, powerful Ossian, head of the Cormac clan and chief of the tuath, slid from his pony and crumpled to the ground.

The druid swirled around to face the rider waiting in the chariot, gold torques gleaming on his neck and wrists.

'Morgor of the clan of Niall,' Faelán rasped, 'claim your right!'

The rider leapt from the chariot, and Ket cried out as he pounced on Ossian and plunged a dagger towards his chest.

'Worm of Cormac, do you surrender?' He crouched over his victim, a handful of scarlet cloak twisted in his fist, the blade hovering.

Ket felt a swelling in his own chest that seemed to push against his throat, squeezing it tight. There was no sound. Not even the breathing of the wind. Then the fallen man gave a feeble nod of his head.

Morgor slashed. The cloak fell from Ossian's shoulders, and splayed out beneath him like a pool of blood.

A grey-robed girl stepped forward, her fingers strumming a harp. To the ripple of music, the druid began to sing. This time his voice was sweet as honey.

'Morgor the Good
Rich and generous

Morgor the Good
Fair in judgement
Morgor the Good
Head of the Niall clan
And chief of the tuath!'

Triumphantly, Morgor sheathed his dagger. The battle was over.

Suddenly everyone was cheering – even the Cormacs. 'Long live Morgor our chieftain!' they shouted.

And the little boy, alone on the ramparts, stared at the druid with awe.

First Test

The morning after the omen, the fosterlings waited, bubbling with nervous excitement, for Faelán to join them.

'At last, we're going to learn some magic!'

Nath-í shook his branch of bronze bells. 'I can't believe it!'

'When I saw that raven, I was so scared!'

'Uch!' Nath-í dived to the ground and scrabbled among the fallen leaves. 'I've dropped one of my bells,' he moaned, standing up and shaking his head.

'Never mind,' said Nessa. 'You've still got all the others.'

'Master Faelán will never choose me,' said Nath-í gloomily. 'I'm too clumsy.'

At his words, they all fell silent, inspecting each other.

'Who will he choose, really?' whispered Riona. Her eyes were like dark pools in her small, worried face.

Ket waited, tense and hopeful, for someone to point to him.

'He said we'll have to do tasks,' said Lorccán. 'Maybe we'll have to fight a battle!'

'Then Nessa'll win for sure,' said Riona. 'She's the best at swordwork and slingshot and . . .'

'Rubbish,' mumbled Nessa.

'But druids don't fight with weapons, do they?' asked Nath-í. 'They use magic.'

'I can do that crane stance Faelán does for a spell,' cried Lorccán. 'Watch!' Eagerly, he raised one leg off the ground.

'Huh, anyone can do that,' retorted Bran, lifting his leg too.

As they both stood there wobbling, Bran wiry and freckled, with ears sticking out from the sides of his head like the handles of an ale cup, and Lorccán pink-cheeked and proud, Riona burst into a fit of giggles.

'You two look like dogs, not cranes!' she sputtered, and they all started to laugh.

'Hush!' said Nessa. 'Faelán's coming!'

The druid emerged from the trees dressed like a king. His full-length robe was not of flax or wool, but soft, shimmering silk. It was dyed in woad blue, the same deep hue as a twilight sky. That was a colour that only a king or a druid was permitted to wear. The morning sun glinted off golden ornaments about his neck and wrists, and the jewelled harp in his arms. But his feet were bare, and when he walked he seemed not to disturb the grass or leaves beneath him. Ket watched longingly. It was almost as though the druid did not touch the ground.

'Will I ever learn to walk like that?' wondered Ket.

Nessa danced impatiently, pigtails twitching and jingling, as the druid crossed the clearing. He passed the campfire, the altar stone with the dry brown stains of blood, and the heaps of heather scattered with rawhide rugs that served as beds.

At last he reached the Sacred Yew where the fosterlings waited. He rested his harp against the tree and lowered himself beside the ogham rod. Bangles clinked along his arms as he steepled long, knobbly fingers.

'Today,' he announced, 'you will memorise a tale.'

'*Storytelling?*' squawked Bran. 'But . . .'

The druid's eyes narrowed.

'I thought we were going to learn secrets,' said Bran gruffly.

'Words,' said Faelán sternly, 'are power.'

Ket thought of the words, all those years ago, that had defeated his father in battle.

'The value of stories is beyond measure,' Faelán continued. 'Tales hold the history of our people and our land. If you become a druid it will be your duty to pass them on to the next generation. Now, which of you has a good memory?'

'Me!' cried Lorccán. 'I can remember anything.'

'Hmm.' Faelán raised one eyebrow. He slid off one of his bangles and laid it on the ground in front of him. 'Watch,' he said.

He placed his knife beside the bracelet, then two small stones, an oak leaf, and a feather. 'And . . .' He looked around. 'These.' A half-melted candle, a limpet shell, and a wisp of tinder were added to the strange array. 'That will do.'

'What are they for?' demanded Lorccán.

Faelán smiled. 'Lend me your cloak.' He held the cape of badger skins in the air. 'Thrice times three are the objects here,' he said. 'You have seen them all, but now . . .' He lowered the cloak over the top. 'Try to name them.'

'Two stones!' shouted Lorccán. 'An oak leaf, a knife, a bangle, a . . . a . . .' He screwed up his face.

'A candle,' whispered Nessa.

'Some tinder,' said Ket.

'That's seven.'

Faelán waited.

Lorccán glared at the lumpy cloak, then Faelán whisked it into the air and they all groaned.

'We forgot the limpet shell and the feather,' Riona exclaimed.

'Ha!' Bran punched Lorccán on the shoulder. 'You're not as brilliant as you thought.'

The druid frowned. 'Take care how you speak,' he reproved. 'Words of scorn or ridicule can destroy another person. We do not use them lightly.'

'Sorry, Master Faelán.' Bran lowered his head, but Ket could see a smile at the corner of his mouth.

'And so . . .' Faelán smoothed down his beard. 'Your first tale – the legend of the Battle of Moytura. This morning the telling of the tale will be mine. But tonight you fosterlings will share it amongst you.' The druid leaned back against the Sacred Yew. 'When you tell a tale,' he said, 'always call for the help of the spirits. The spirit of this tree has existed so long, she has witnessed not only the telling but the birth of legends. She has seen the heroes, the victories, the deaths and defeats. Her roots link her to the depths of the Underworld and her branches to the height of the sky. Touch her, and feel the spirit.'

The fosterlings eyed each other. It seemed now as if the gnarled, sinewy yew might writhe into life. The tree had three trunks, ancient and twisted, and it was so wide that if all six fosterlings had stood in a ring, they could barely have circled it with their clasped hands. Tentatively, they reached out and laid their palms against the bark.

'I can feel something, I can feel something!' yelled Lorccán.

'You *would*,' muttered Bran.

Ket screwed his eyes shut. Over hundreds of years, many people must have touched this tree. For a fleeting instant he sensed their presence, as if they were around him, watching.

'Now for the tale,' said Faelán.

One by one, he turned to each of them and spoke their names.

'Nath-í?'

Nath-í leaned earnestly forward, wriggling, so that his knobbly elbows and knees bumped the others.

'Bran?' asked Faelán. Bran was punching Nath-í's knee and didn't hear. 'Bran!' Faelán repeated.

Bran looked up.

'Lorccán . . .'

Lorccán stuck out his chest. '*I'm* listening,' he said.

'Ket,' said the druid. Ket stared back. He was too excited to speak. His heart felt like a trapped bird, flapping wildly against the net that held it.

Faelán turned to the girls.

'Riona?' Riona pressed her fingers over her mouth.

'And Nessa.' Nessa smiled and smoothed her skirt

over her knees. She had a heart-shaped face and when her mouth quirked up in a smile, her chin grew more pointy.

'Listen well,' said Faelán. 'Fortune favours those who recount a tale faithfully.' He picked up his harp and strummed a few notes, then began, part in song, and part in chant. 'Long, long ago, there were people called the Tuatha de Danaan who dwelt far to the north, in Falias, Gorias, Murias and Findias.'

Faelán's voice and the strumming of the harp had a magical power. Ket found himself drifting into the world of the story. He felt the bobbing of the silver boat, heard the sound of waves and the slapping of oars as Elatha, King of the Fomoria, sailed towards the land of the Tuatha de Danaan. He saw the beauteous Princess Eriu with her long golden hair coming out to greet him.

'One day, the Tuatha de Danaan set out in a fleet of boats to capture the land of the Fir Bolg . . . this very land where we live now.'

The druid swept out his arm, and Ket stared around, trying to see with the eyes of a stranger. The campsite was a clearing surrounded by trees. In the centre, a cauldron simmered over a fire. There was no furniture, walls or roof, though the druid and his followers had dwelled here for many years. Logs and rocks served as seats, and the beds were soft boughs covered with animal skins.

Stretching to the south and east, a forest of birch, ash and rowan glowed with leaves of red and gold. Around the fosterlings, the trees thinned out and beyond their trunks could be seen a sward of grass with stony grey outcrops. A river meandered across the plain and trickled away in a haze of purple heather. In the distance, where the ground was low and marshy, the ringforts of Nessa's clan were visible, but the other farms of the tuath were out of sight, beyond the forest and the hills.

'The plain of Moytura,' Faelán went on, 'is where they fought their battle. It is drenched with their blood.'

In silence, the fosterlings stared between the trees, trying to imagine the green grass strewn with the bodies of dead and wounded. Above their heads, the dark, brooding shape of the Sacred Yew stretched out branches of evil-smelling needles.

'And that cairn,' Faelán pointed, 'is the burial mound for the Tuatha de Danaan who were killed in the battle. It is heaped with one stone for every de Danaan who died.' Ket gazed at the huge pile of white stones in the middle of the plain. There were hundreds of them. *Thousands* of them. 'But that mound is not only stones.' Faelán's voice sank to a whisper. 'There are skulls there, too – the severed heads of those they conquered . . . and slaughtered.'

'Eeuugh!' Riona shuddered.

Faelán paused a moment before he spoke again. 'That tomb is an entrance to the Underworld, where all dead heroes live in immortality. The Tuatha de Danaan have not really perished. They are still there, deep inside the tomb. We call them the Shadow Ones.'

Six pairs of eyes widened.

'And that monument there . . .' Faelán gestured to a tall pillar stone standing alone on a hillock, 'marks the place where the hand of Nuada, King of the Tuatha de Danaan, was struck from his arm by an enemy sword!'

Ket gulped and wrapped a hand around his own wrist.

'Who won the battle?' demanded Lorccán.

Faelán smiled. 'The Fir Bolg were mighty fighters, but the Tuatha de Danaan had sages who kept a secret lore, and practised magic arts. They were greater far than all other sages.'

'The druids!' breathed Ket.

'The druids,' Faelán agreed. 'By the power of their magic arts, the Tuatha De Danaan gained victory in battle.'

'What happened to King Nuada?'

'Credne the Smith fashioned him a new hand out of silver, but now Nuada had a blemish and according to the laws of the Tuatha de Danaan he was no longer fit for kingship.'

From the corner of his eye, Ket saw Nath-í touch the purple birthmark on his cheek.

'A new sovereign was chosen,' said Faelán, 'Eochu the Beautiful, son of Eriu and Elatha. It was the Tuatha de Danaan who named our land Eriu, for the mother of Eochu. They brought us the laws of kingship. And . . .' he rose to his feet, 'the secrets of the druids – those secrets I propose to pass on to you.'

He scanned their upturned faces.

'To *one* of you,' he corrected. 'One of you will learn the secret of how to foretell from the stars which is the most auspicious day to travel, or harvest, or . . .' he broke into a smile, 'become an anruth. To one of you only will I teach the poetic strains of the harp, cures for the sick, the rules of judgement . . .'

He broke off.

'Choose your portions and learn them well,' he said sternly. 'Your time of trial begins.'

The Telling

'Here they come!' The two anruth twins, Art and Bronal, bounced excitedly, identical mops of fair hair flopping up and down.

Goll and Maura, the two older anruth, turned to watch as the fosterlings filed towards them. Ket held up his branch of bells, grinning proudly, but Nath-í stumbled along scarlet with embarrassment, and plonked himself by the side of the fire, his spindly arms and legs sticking out awkwardly like a bundle of twigs.

'So.' Faelán the Druid leaned forward. 'Let us see what you young ones have managed to learn.'

'All of it!' cried Lorccán eagerly. 'I could tell the whole story on my own!'

'And perchance next time you shall,' said the druid. 'But tonight you are only required to say your part. Now, let us hear the tale of the Battle of Moytura. Who will commence?'

Nath-í shifted nervously.

'Ring your bells then,' said Faelán, 'and remember, fortune favours those who recount a tale faithfully.'

Everyone tensed as Nath-í jiggled his branch, but none of the bells fell off. With earnest concentration, he began.

'Long ago, there were people called the Tuatha de Danaan. They dwelt far to the north, in Falias, Gorias, Murias and . . .' Panic flashed across his face, but then he grinned. 'Findias!' he finished on a note of triumph.

The druid stroked his moustache.

'Who's next?'

Nessa raised her hand and gave her bells a firm shake.

'There was a princess of the Tuatha de Danaan,' she recited. 'Her name was Eriu.' Nessa's words were clear and confident. 'One day Eriu saw, sailing out of the sea, a boat of silver. Out from the boat stepped a man arrayed in gold and jewels. He was Elatha, King of the Fomoria.

'He lingered with Eriu one hour, and when he rose to leave, Eriu wept.

'"Grieve not," said the King of the Fomoria, "for you shall bear my son." He drew from his finger a ring of gold and placed it in her hand. "Call my son Eochu the Beautiful," he said.'

Nessa had barely finished when Lorccán was ringing his bells. 'My turn!' he yelled. He leapt to his feet and braced himself, legs apart.

'The Tuatha de Danaan set out for battle!' he announced. 'And they had the best sword in the whole world. The Sword of Nuada. If someone drew that sword, everyone else was *dead*!' Lorccán swung his arm, making a swishing noise. 'And that wasn't all. They had the Spear of Lug too, a spear that never missed.' He pretended to stab himself in the chest then gurgled and jerked dramatically.

Ket saw Bronal roll his eyes at his twin.

'Get on with it, Lorccán,' he muttered, 'don't be such a show-off.'

'And they had this stone,' said Lorccán. 'The Stone of Fal. When the right person stood on it, it yelled out, and everyone knew that person must be the Ard Ri, the true High King. And they never got hungry because they had the Cauldron of Dagda, that never emptied!

'There!' He plopped back in his place, beaming. 'I told you I could do it! Go on, Ket, your turn.'

Ket took a breath and stumbled to his feet. His heart was pumping so hard it felt like a beating drum. All around, expectant faces leaned towards him. They looked hollowed and ghoulish in the firelight.

'Go on,' repeated Lorccán.

Ket looked back at him in blank horror. The words were gone. There was nothing in his mind, nothing!

'He can't do it. He's forgotten it,' crowed Bran.

Tears of rage and humiliation seared Ket's eyes. He cast a desperate glance around, then plunged towards the blackness of the forest.

Voices from the Past

Branches tore his face and hair, but Ket felt only the stabbing in his heart. Running blindly, he tripped on a fallen log and crashed to the ground. He sprawled there with his face in the dirt, too stricken even to lift his head. Despair surged through him. The memory of himself as a little child, pleading to be a druid, hammered at his brain. In his mind he could see himself back in the ringfort standing beside his father.

'I should have died a hero in the battle,' Ossian was muttering. 'I should have gone out in a blaze of glory, and been worthy to join my ancestors.'

'But aren't you going to fight Morgor and be the chieftain again?' the young boy asked.

'With that druid's spell on my head? I can never rule again.'

'What about fighting the druid then?' asked Ket.

'The druid?' Ossian lifted his doleful face, and gave a watery smile. 'My child, I could no more fight a druid than I could take up arms against the sun or the rain or the wind.'

'Aren't you angry at him, though?'

Ossian shook his head. 'Do we feel anger at rain or wind when they make us cold and wet? Of course not. For they are far beyond the touch of our mortal emotions. And the druid has greater power still, for the rain and wind obey his command.'

The little Ket stood for a moment, thinking. 'Can druids do *anything*?' he asked.

'Anything,' Ossian assented. 'They can foretell the future. They can speak to the dead. Druids control the world.'

Uncle Ailbe stamped up and rested a heavy hand on Ket's shoulder. 'This first-born son of yours is growing fast. Too old now to be living with his mother, eh?'

Ket watched anxiously as his mother straightened her back and blew a stray lock of hair out of her eyes.

'Yes,' Úna answered, 'he'll be seven at Samhain; time for him to leave for his foster home.'

'Aha, thought so,' Ailbe boomed. 'So, what are your plans for him?'

Úna glanced at her husband.

'He was due to join his cousin Ross.' Ossian's words were slow and harsh. 'Ragallach's a kind foster father. He'd promised Ket a fine silver scabbard, fit for a chieftain's son, and his own pony. But now . . .'

He spread his hands in bewilderment.

'Ach, Ragallach'll still make him welcome.' Ailbe's voice was loud and hearty. 'And you'll enjoy being with your cousin, won't you, young Ket?'

But little Ket didn't want to leave his family at all, and move to a strange ringfort.

'Why can't I just stay here?' he mumbled.

Auntie Mell patted his head. 'Don't worry, Ket, every child of seven leaves home to be a fosterling. You'll be fine.'

'We've all done it.' Uncle Senach was talking now. 'You'll learn to split wood, mend fences, do the weeding . . . it'll make a man of you.'

Ket stared at him in dismay. Weed? Chop? Then it dawned on him. Now he was no longer a chieftain's son, he would have to do all the chores of a commoner.

'You'll learn to be a brave, strong man, and one day you can go a-hosting and regain the lordship for the Cormacs.' Auntie Mell beamed at him. 'One day you'll wear the red cloak of a chieftain.'

As she spoke, Ket saw in his mind the puddle of cloak beneath his father's fallen body, and the leering face of Morgor. But clearest of all, he remembered the awe-inspiring figure of the druid.

'But I don't want to be a chieftain,' he said. 'I want to be a druid.'

'You funny little fellow!' Uncle Ailbe let out a chuckle and gave Ket a playful clip on the ear.

Auntie Mell chortled too, her round cheeks wobbling. 'And how would you do the magic?'

Everyone in the room was laughing now. Ket could feel his face growing hot. 'The druid will teach me,' he growled. 'I'll go and live with the druid and be *his* foster son. Then I can learn to do magic instead of stupid things like herding pigs and chopping wood.'

'Enough of this foolishness.' Úna gripped his shoulder and began to drag a comb through his hair. 'It is all arranged. Tomorrow you go as foster son to Ragallach. You'll learn to be a fine farmer, and when you're old enough he'll teach you how to wield a sword and go on hostings.'

Ket wrenched his head away and stamped his foot. 'Swords are stupid!' he cried. 'They weren't any use to Father! He lost the last battle, *and* his lordship . . .'

'Ket!' Úna's voice was sharp, her face white and shocked.

Guiltily, Ket glanced over his shoulder and saw Father standing with his head bowed. Ket's stomach twisted in shame.

But Ossian was not angry. 'Ket is right,' he sighed. 'The best champions and the finest swords are no defence against magic.'

Ket flew across the room and threw his arms around his father.

'Then you'll let me go as foster son to the druid?!'

Ossian held his son in front of him. 'It is true, a druid is more powerful than a chieftain. More powerful even than a king. For no one can rule unless a druid wills it.' Ossian turned to his wife. 'Úna, why should our son not learn to be a druid?'

'Because druids live in the forest like wild beasts,' Úna expostulated. 'They don't even have houses!'

Bríd was capering around, squealing in delight. 'Ket's going to sleep on the ground, and eat leaves off the trees!' she chortled.

Was that true? Ket glanced anxiously at his father.

'My boy doesn't need cosseting,' Ossian growled. 'He can stand a bit of cold and hunger. He's tough.'

The little boy looked at the warm blankets heaped on the beds, the steaming cauldron, and the cosy flicker of the fire. He listened to the muffled sound of rain outside, pattering against the thatch.

There was a scared, cold feeling in the pit of his stomach, but he stuck out his jaw and looked back at his father.

'Yes, I can do it,' he vowed.

ogham

'And I did!' Ket raised his face from the forest floor and cried out in anguish. 'For five years I've slept on the ground, and eaten leaves. But what is the use of it, if the druid is going to send me away?'

Above him, the tall shapes of the trees towered silently.

'Draw out the strength from the Spirit of the Tree,' he heard the words of the druid.

Ket flopped against the nearest trunk, and waited, but all he could feel was the hardness of the bark.

Then the ground tremored; he heard feet tramping through the undergrowth, and a voice calling his name. The bobbing flame of a torch came and went between the trees, and the next moment Goll was standing in front of him. The anruth's earnest face and long, sandy locks shone in a circle of light, but the rest of him blended into the shadows.

'I did learn it,' said Ket defensively. 'Really I did. I knew it off by heart.'

'I know,' said Goll.

Ket gazed at the tip of his shoe in the flickering pool of torchlight.

'I remember it perfectly now.'

'Go on then, say it.'

'The Tuatha de Danaan, led by their king, Nuada, set out in a fleet of boats to capture the land of the Fir Bolg. In the battle, the hand of King Nuada was struck from his arm; and though Credne the Smith fashioned a new hand of silver, Nuada had a blemish and was no longer fit for kingship.'

'Well done!'

'But I couldn't say it when everyone was watching me. I failed the first test! At the next new moon . . .' He saw himself cowering, shamed, under the druid's gaze. 'Faelán will send me away.'

'Would that be so terrible?' asked Goll. 'If you go back to your clan you can polish up your fighting skills and one day you can lead the Cormacs into battle. You can become a chieftain like your father was.'

'But chieftains don't have powers like the druids!'

protested Ket. 'Chieftains can't talk to the dead, or . . . or read the stars, or *any* of the things that Faelán can do. My father thought he was special when he put on grand banquets, and sat and watched while everyone else did the dirty work, but . . . but . . . all the time he was just an ordinary man. And *now* . . .' Ket thought of Ossian, lined and weary, fingernails grimed with dirt, and his voice cracked in despair. 'It's only the druids who have real power.'

Goll rubbed his chin.

'Well then,' he said at last. 'You'd better go back and say your part of the tale. They're all waiting for you. Maura served out the muck-weed stew to keep them occupied. But Bran,' he grinned, 'is getting impatient.'

Ket had a momentary image of that freckled face with its derisive grin and wild mop of hair the colour of a flaming sunset.

He eyed Goll worriedly. 'What if I forget again?' he asked in a small voice.

'You won't. This time I'll show you some feda to help you remember.'

'Feda?'

'You know, ogham signs.'

'But . . . you're not allowed to do that, are you?'

'Why not? Faelán gave you permission to learn them if you can find them out. And as an anruth I'm obliged to be helpful and sharing. So . . .' He shrugged. 'I'll only show you a bit, though, just enough to help you with the story. These ones might not even be in the message.' Goll pulled out his knife and scratched a line on the trunk of a tree. 'That's a stemline,' he said. 'You can draw a line like this or you can just use the edge of a stone. Some feda go left of the stemline, and some go right.' Moving upwards from the bottom of the tree trunk, he started to draw little marks on each side of the line. 'And some go right across, and some slope like hills . . .' Ket watched in bewilderment as scratches appeared all over the trunk, white against the grey-green of the bark. 'But now let's do the ones you need to know.' Goll looked at Ket and frowned.

'Nuada,' he said. 'That's the first important word in your story. You need *nuin*, the *n* sound, for Nuada. Five strokes pointing right.' He drew *n* on the tree.

'What did Nuada do?' he asked.

'He led a battle.'

'Good,' said Goll, 'and what happened in the battle?'

'He lost his hand.'

'Then here's *huathe*, *h*, for hand.' Above *nuin*,

Goll drew another feda, just one stroke to the left. 'There.'

He leaned back on his heels. 'Now, show me how the feda tell the story.'

Ket pointed to *nuin.* '*N* is for writing Nuada,' he said. 'Nuada led the Tuatha de Danaan in a battle. And . . .' He grinned and pointed excitedly to the other feda. 'And *h.* That's for hand. Nuada lost his hand so he couldn't be king any more! Now, *I'll* draw the feda.' He grabbed the knife and tried to scratch a sign in the trunk. It was harder than it looked, but at last he achieved five flat strokes. 'There! Nuin!'

'Don't forget to put the stemline in. On the left,' warned Goll. 'Otherwise it could be *quert* or *iodo.*'

But Ket was impatient to return to the others. 'Come on!' He bounded to his feet. 'I can go back and tell the story now. If we draw the feda on . . . on a stick or something . . .'

Goll chuckled. 'It'll be quicker to write them the secret way,' he said.

'What secret way?'

'Watch my hands.'

Ket looked down. Goll's hands were curled in fists. Then his right hand flicked open for a moment and closed again. 'How many fingers did I point?' he demanded.

'One.'

Goll nodded. 'One stroke pointing left. Which feda is that?'

'*Huathe*! *H* for hand. And here's *n* for Nuada.' Ket opened and closed his own hand, pointing all five fingers.

'Look who's back,' Art announced, as Ket, following Goll, stepped sheepishly out of the forest.

'Don't worry, Ket. We waited for you. We didn't finish the tale without you,' called Riona.

There was a stir of expectation as everyone set down their bowls and turned to face him. Nessa's eyes were anxious and encouraging.

'Have the trees brought you wisdom?' inquired Faelán.

'The trees? Uuuh . . .' In his mind's eye Ket saw the ogham carved into the bark. 'Yes, the trees, of course!' he replied. He stooped and picked up his branch of bells. Goll was holding out five pointing fingers. Ket grinned, and gave the bells a shake. 'Nuada!' he announced. 'King Nuada led the Tuatha de Danaan in a battle. And then . . .' He glanced at Goll's single pointing finger. '*H*. . . hand!' He looked round the circle, light-headed with relief. 'The hand of King Nuada was struck from his arm; and though

Credne the Smith fashioned a new hand of silver, Nuada had a blemish and was no longer fit for kingship. There!' He turned to Bran. 'Now your turn.'

But as Bran began to speak, Ket's eyes drifted to the ogham rod Faelán had stuck in the ground. At the very top there was one straight line pointing left. *Huathe! H* for hand! He already knew the first feda in the message!

The Greater Harmony

'So,' said the druid next morning, 'Ket has already benefited from my first instruction, to gain strength and inspiration from the trees.'

Ket squirmed as the others turned to look at him. 'Well,' he mumbled. 'I . . .'

'Now you must build on that lesson,' Faelán continued. 'You must all build. You must study and communicate with everything around you, from the tallest tree to the smallest insect. Open your eyes and your ears. Be receptive to the spirits around you. See, listen, hear what they have to tell you. Come with me now, look around. Tell me what you see.'

He strode towards the forest and the fosterlings hurried after him.

'Trees!' called Lorccán.

'Ah.' The druid paused below the hollow oak. 'But what are the messages from the trees?' The fosterlings looked at each other blankly. 'How do they tell us the end of the year approaches?' probed Faelán.

'Their leaves are changing colour.'

'And falling off!' cried Bran, holding out his hand to catch an oak leaf as it floated down. Before it could reach him, Lorccán dived forward and plucked it from the air.

'Got it!' he yelled.

'Ah, Lorccán,' Faelán chuckled, 'you have just won yourself good health during the coming months of cold. Now, what other signs tell us that winter is approaching?'

They stared round for inspiration 'If it were summer, what would you see?' asked Faelán.

'*Green* leaves,' said Lorccán quickly.

'Flowers.'

'Pigs rooting for acorns,' said Nessa, 'and the swineherds who bring them from the ringforts.'

Ket closed his eyes and pictured the woodland in the month of Beltane. The trees and bushes would be festive with bloom – cascades of white on the hawthorn and rowan, bright sprays of yellow on the gorse, golden catkins dangling from the oak tree, bluebells nodding their heads. He could feel the sun warm through the branches and hear the buzz of insects.

'Bees and butterflies,' he murmured.

'And what else can you hear?' asked Faelán.

'Pipits, reed warblers, swallows.'

'Good.' Ket opened his eyes and Faelán nodded, pleased. 'But now . . .' The druid swept out his arms. 'All those signs of summer have gone. What do you see now in the forest?'

'The blackberries are ripe,' said Lorccán.

'And the sloe berries, and the dark purple elderberries.'

'Hazelnuts,' said Nessa. 'The squirrels are gathering their winter hoards.'

'But that stuff's all obvious,' Bran broke in. 'Everyone knows trees lose their leaves in autumn, and berries are ready to pick. You don't have to be a druid for that!'

'Ah, so that is why *you* seek further.' Faelán stooped and patted the rotting leaf litter. 'Search beneath these leaves . . .' He thrust his hand under the leaves and when he drew it out, a grey, scaly woodlouse was crawling across his palm. 'Hold out your hand,' he instructed Riona.

She pulled a face as he eased the insect onto her reluctant finger.

'What can you feel?' he inquired.

'Nothing.'

'This insect is so small, so light, we cannot feel it exists. Most people would crush it, and not even be aware they did so. But in spite of its tiny size, it plays an important part in the cycle of life. By nibbling the fallen leaves, it will gradually break them down till they become part of the soil. In turn, the dead leaves will nourish the tree that bore them, so that new leaves can grow.' He looked up into the branches of the oak then back at his listeners. His tone changed and he snapped a question. 'What are the lessons in this?'

Nessa gestured in excitement. Her green eyes shone, and her red-gold hair was the same glowing colour as the birch leaves.

'We can all do something to help others, even if we are small and weak,' she exclaimed.

'Good.'

'And . . . and we should respect all lives, even the lives of insects?' asked Ket.

Faelán nodded. 'Insects, trees, even leaves. Ordinary mortals smash through this world, disturbing and destroying for their own needs. But a druid tries to be part of the Greater Harmony.'

'I've seen that when you walk,' said Ket excitedly. 'Your feet don't even disturb the grass. Are you going to teach us to walk like that?'

The druid tugged his beard. 'That is something you must work out for yourselves,' he said. 'It is learnt through observation. Between now and the next new moon, I advise you to open your eyes and look around you.' He spread his arms. 'Study the insects; the birds; the buds on the trees. The river. The sky. Respect them, and learn what they can teach.'

'But . . .'

The druid dropped his hands. 'Yes, Bran?'

'We've already got all those stories to learn!'

'If you memorise the tales, the poems and the songs, and learn nothing more,' chided Faelán, 'then you will only reach the level of a bard. Is that your desire? It is an honourable calling, but a bard has not the powers of a druid.'

'I want to be a druid,' mumbled Bran.

'Well then, keep your eyes and your ears open. Look around you – in daytime and at night, in sunshine and in rain – and you will learn many important things.'

Gently, he returned the woodlouse to the leaves, and straightened up.

'Ket . . .' He turned. 'You have already shown an affinity with the trees. Which tree was it that gave you support when you needed to complete your story task?'

'Uuh . . .' Ket saw all the others watching him, jealous and curious. He closed his eyes and pictured the ogham signs scraped into the smooth, grey-green trunk. 'It was an ash.'

'An *ash*?!' The druid's voice rose inquiringly. 'The ash is a warrior's tree. Its strong wood makes fine spears, but I would not have expected . . .'

He gazed at Ket, one eyebrow raised, and Ket felt his cheeks burn with embarrassment.

'It wasn't the tree that helped me, exactly,' he mumbled. 'It was Goll. He showed me some ogham. He carved it on the trunk.'

'Aaah!' Faelán nodded, but Ket could feel the indignation of the others around him.

'Is . . . is Goll *allowed* to help?' burst out Riona.

'Why not?' responded Faelán. 'When I challenged you to search for ogham clues I did not tell you where or how to look. It is your good fortune if one of the anruth chooses to teach you. But now . . .' The corner of his mouth curled. 'Ket has a difficult choice. He must decide if he will share his knowledge with the rest of you.' In the strained silence that followed, he turned to leave.

The moment he was out of sight, the others rounded on Ket.

'You cheated,' cried Lorccán indignantly.

'Ooh, Master Faelán, the *trees* helped me,' mimicked Bran.

'You *are* going to share, Ket, aren't you?' pleaded Riona.

'Will you?' asked Nath-í.

'Of course he won't,' scoffed Bran.

'Hey, everyone, stop pestering him,' scolded Nessa. 'We're all competing, remember. He doesn't have to tell.'

'I . . .' Ket had planned to tell Nessa anyway. And maybe Nath-í and Riona. But as for Lorccán and Bran . . . Ket pressed his lips together. If those two found clues, they would never dream of sharing. But Bran had a point. Faelán had just told them that being a druid was all about helping others.

'He's going to tell! He's going to tell!' squealed Riona as Ket knelt on the ground and began to brush some leaves aside. 'Careful, don't hurt the woodlice!' she warned.

'I need a clear space,' said Ket.

Everyone hovered over him as he scraped the shape of a feda in the dirt.

'That's an *n* sound, for Nuada.'

'Is it in the message?' blurted Lorccán. 'I'm going to see.'

'Bet you're tricking us,' said Bran.

The two of them leapt to their feet and raced towards the ogham stick.

'But . . .' Bemused, Ket leaned back on his heels. 'They should have waited,' he said. 'I know another one too.'

Riona squirmed excitedly.

'Show us. Quick!' she said. 'Before they come back.'

She gathered up the leaves again, and as soon as Ket had drawn *huathe*, she covered it up, glancing over her shoulder. 'Don't let them see, don't let them see!'

'Hey, *I* didn't see it properly,' Nath-í complained.

'Come on.' Riona grabbed Nessa's hand and tugged her to her feet. 'Let's move away from here. Before they guess what we're doing.'

The girls hurried away, giggling, while Nath-í poked at the pile of leaves.

'Watch out!' Ket had spied a frightened woodlouse scurrying for cover. He tried to coax it onto his finger as Faelán had done, but the instant the creature felt the touch of a hand it curled into a ball.

'It didn't do that when Master Faelán picked it up,' said Ket ruefully.

'It wasn't afraid of Master Faelán,' said Nath-í. Ket lifted the tiny grey ball onto his hand and they both peered at it closely. All they could see was the hard shell. The delicate feet and soft underside were tucked safely inside. 'I wish I had a shell like that,' said Nath-í. 'Imagine! Even if it fell from the top of a tree it wouldn't hurt itself.'

'Faelán told us to study them and learn from them,' said Ket. 'Maybe . . . maybe if we curl up when we fall . . .'

'Like this!' cried Nath-í excitedly. He jumped up, hunched his shoulders, folded his long arms against his chest and bent his knees. Ket thought he looked more like a grasshopper than a woodlouse. 'Okay, push me,' ordered Nath-í.

But when Ket gave him a shove, Nath-í crashed to the ground with a yowl and sat up rubbing his elbow.

'It didn't work,' he grumbled.

'You didn't keep your arms tucked in!' said Ket.

'*You* try keeping your arms in when you're falling,' retorted Nath-í. 'It's not possible. We can't learn anything from stupid beetles.'

He stood up and hobbled off.

'Faelán says we can,' muttered Ket.

He tipped the woodlouse back among the leaves, wrapped his arms around his knees and waited to see what would happen. He could hear the others tramping through the trees. From deep in the forest came the bellow of a stag. Then, just in front of him, a blackbird landed on the ground, and cocked its head.

Ket froze. The bird hopped closer, took a stab at the leaves, tilted its head again, and then, deciding Ket was no threat, began to search busily.

Ket watched intently as the bird burrowed with its beak, flipping and tossing leaves, every now and then lifting its head to gulp something down. It was so close, Ket could see the specks of soil and insect legs sticking to its beak. He could almost feel he had a beak himself. If he wiped his face he would find crumbs of insects on his lips.

Twinges of pain began to pluck at Ket's shoulders. Cautiously, he unlaced his fingers to ease his back. Instantly, the bird let out a peal of alarm, and flew away.

Ket unfolded, and rose stiffly to his feet. As he crossed the clearing he glanced at his reflection in the bucket of water. He almost expected to see a beak growing out of his face. Instead, he saw a boy with hair and eyes the same dusky brown as a skylark's wing.

'And there's dirt all over my clothes and face,' he muttered ruefully. 'That blackbird probably couldn't even see me among the brown bracken.'

Squatting down to wash his face, he paused first, eyeing his reflection, and tried to imagine how he would look wearing a silver circlet round his head, and a long grey robe, like an anruth.

'Hey, what are you gawping at?' Lorccán came sauntering over.

'Nothing.'

Ket splashed water on his face, and jumped up. He scowled at the tall boy with hair of pale, shining gold. It was easy to imagine Lorccán dressed in the garb of an anruth.

That night, when they sat around the fire, Lorccán was bursting with pride.

'Guess what I found!' he said. 'I saw an otter! And I watched how it used its legs in the water. When the weather warms up, I'm going to be the best swimmer of everyone.'

'I looked in the river too, and I searched all over the woods but I didn't see anything,' grumbled Nath-í.

'That's 'cause you crashed along like a herd of cows!' said Bran. 'I found a squirrel and you scared it off.'

'Animals are too hard!' sighed Riona. 'If you try to get close, they run away. I just gave up and looked at the trees. What did you do, Ket?'

'I . . .' Ket was embarrassed. He didn't want to sound boastful like Lorccán. 'I was lucky. A blackbird came feeding right up close to me. I watched it for ages. But I don't think I learnt anything.'

'You probably learnt how to eat worms,' chortled Bran.

'A blackbird!' Riona exclaimed. 'How did you get it to come so close to you?'

'I curled up like this.' Ket hugged his knees. 'And kept still.'

'Like a woodlouse,' said Nath-í.

Ket stared at him. Of course! It wasn't the bird who had taught him a lesson at all, it was the woodlouse. While Nath-í had been crashing around frightening the animals, he, Ket, was learning how to watch without disturbing them. Maybe next he would learn to walk like Faelán!

Samhain Eve

It was the eve of Samhain – the last day of the year, a time of danger and powerful magic. Tonight the Spirits of the Dead would rise from their tombs and search for living bodies to possess.

At the druid's camp, preparations for Samhain were very different from the panic and fear Ket remembered in his father's household. Here there was no frantic gathering-in of crops and livestock, no hiding behind high stone walls. Instead, Faelán ordered the anruth to open the doorway to the burial mound and lay out gifts of nuts and apples to welcome the Spirits of the Dead.

'Now,' he said, addressing the fosterlings, 'go

gather some aspen branches.' He hurried away to check that the apples were washed and polished and all the nuts perfect.

The fosterlings eyed each other. Aspen was used to measure the dead for their graves. The scent of its burning would help to lure their spirits.

Lorccán was the first to speak.

'I'm not afraid. I know where to find an aspen,' he cried, and bounded towards the forest.

The others followed reluctantly.

'I don't like Samhain,' whimpered Riona.

'Here!' called Lorccán. 'Over here!'

He was waiting in front of a tree with a tall, silvery trunk. Above his head, bright yellow leaves trembled and whispered. Dutifully, Nath-í bent to scavenge for fallen twigs. Bran took hold of a lower branch and gave it a tug.

'Bran!' said Nessa. 'You're not allowed to do that!'

Bran snorted. 'Old Feather-cloak can't see me.'

'But . . .'

'Are you going to tell on me?'

'No, of course not. But you're hurting a living tree.'

'So?'

When Bran ripped the branch from the tree, Ket felt uncomfortable, as if he was watching someone tear out another person's hair. He fumbled for the red band Auntie Mell had tied around his wrist all those years ago, that last Samhain before he left home. He rubbed the worn, frayed strands between his fingers and felt comforted. The red dye, colour of fire and blood, would bring him protection.

'I'm going to find some holly,' said Nessa. 'Come on, Ket, come and help me.'

The fosterlings would spend the dreadful night of Samhain cowering inside the hollow oak, hoping that red berries and spiky leaves hung around the tree would ward off evil spirits.

As Ket and Nessa threaded their way through the forest, they came upon a man from the ringforts lopping branches from a holly tree.

Nessa called a greeting, and then her face lit up as the man turned. 'Uncle Tirech!' She ran towards him. 'How's everyone at the ringfort? How's Mother? And all my cousins?'

'Nay, no time to gossip now, Nessa!' The man shook his head. 'I've lots to do before sunset!' He glanced at his basket of holly. 'That'll do,' he muttered, and looking harassed, he tramped off through the forest.

Nessa watched his departing back with disappointment.

'Come on, Nessa. Look at all the leaves and berries he's dropped on the ground,' said Ket, gathering them up.

As the fosterlings headed back to camp, loaded with boughs of aspen and holly, the scent of baking barm-brack cakes wafted towards them. Ket and Nath-í looked round for Goll. As eldest sons, they were obliged to carry cakes as offerings to the tombs of their ancestors.

Goll met them by the fire, where Maura was laying lumps of dough to cook on a heated stone. Her cheeks were red as the holly berries from the effort of kneading, and her stiff, straw-coloured hair stuck out in all directions from the silver fillet that circled her head. She flipped the cakes over, then lifted two and laid them on pieces of bark.

Nath-í rubbed his belly wistfully. 'Can I eat one now?' he asked. Spindly and fast-growing as a fox-glove flower, he was always hungry.

Maura shook her head. 'When you come back.' She slapped another lump of dough on the stone. 'I'm making plenty.'

Nath-í held the fresh-baked cake to his nose and gave a longing sniff, then set off holding it gingerly.

'Try not to drop it!' Maura called after him.

Nath-í headed for the hills, for his clan lands were in the north, and Goll took the path across the plain down to the marshes.

Ket waited impatiently for the next cake, his stomach gurgling as the hot, sweet aroma filled his nostrils. At last his offering was ready. He curled the bark carefully around it, and hurried into the forest. The sooner he returned, the sooner he could sink his teeth into one of those golden rounds sticky with dark chunks of bilberry.

The Cormac ancestors lay buried in a clearing in the forest. The tall stone pillars that circled their mound cast long shadows. As Ket stepped into the clearing, he saw that the flat slab of stone set in the side of the grass-covered mound had been pushed aside.

'Father!' he called in a loud whisper.

Ossian emerged, and waved. He was stooped now, and almost bald.

'Fáilte!' he replied. 'Still no anruth robes?' He gestured at Ket's short brown tunic.

'No, but soon, maybe.' In an eager undertone, Ket told Ossian about the challenge. 'Master Faelán is going to judge us, and choose one of us to be an anruth.'

'I'm sure he'll choose you,' said Ossian, patting his shoulder. 'But if he doesn't, no matter, Ragallach will still take you. Now . . .' He held out a hand. 'You've brought the offering, I see.'

Ket hesitated. 'Should I do it myself?'

'Time enough when you're older,' said Ossian.

Ket nodded with relief. 'When I'm a druid, nothing will frighten me! And I'll know all sorts of spells to protect me.'

'But you must pay your respects to your ancestors out here,' his father reminded him.

As Ossian crouched down to ease his way back through the low portal, Ket turned reluctantly to the white stones standing sentinel around the grave. Slowly, he began to move around, resting his hands on each pillar. The stones were cool and moist and it seemed to Ket as if the coldness and heaviness of death were seeping inside his own skin.

The tallest and broadest pillar was Grandfather Cormac's memorial. Orange lichen dappled the bleached surface, and marks, half worn away by age and weather, were etched up one side.

Ket stretched out his hand, then stopped, transfixed. Of course! Those marks were feda, just like Faelán had carved in the birch rod!

'Ogham,' he whispered, shaking with excitement. He looked round wildly for something to copy them on. There was a flat stone near his foot, half-buried in the earth. He scrabbled it out, and using a piece of sharp rock, started to scratch the word on its surface.

'Well, that's done then.' Startled by the sound of Ossian's voice, Ket almost stabbed his own hand. 'Better get home . . .' Ossian's voice sharpened. 'What are you *doing*, Ket?'

Ket scrambled to his feet. 'Sorry, no time to tell you now!' he blurted. 'Got to go!'

Hugging the precious clue to his chest, he turned and sped back to camp.

Nearing the sound of voices and the scent of aspen smoke, Ket forced himself to slow down and saunter into camp. Lorccán and Bran must never guess his secret.

'Hey,' called Nessa. 'What took you so long?'

The fosterlings were clustered around the hollow oak, draping it with holly to keep out evil spirits.

'Yes, hurry, it's getting late,' cried Riona. She was on her knees, laying a ring of prickly leaves and red berries around the roots of the tree.

'Coming,' said Ket. 'I'll just . . . I'll just . . .'

At that moment, there was a loud hiss and billow of smoke and Art and Bronal staggered away from the fire, coughing and flapping their hands. Ket grinned with delight. On Samhain Eve every flame in the land had to be extinguished, and the two anruth had just poured water over their campfire.

Masked by the pall of smoke, Ket crept over to the Sacred Yew and squatted beside the ogham rod. He laid his stone on the ground and examined it eagerly.

The word had to be *Cormac*, his grandfather's name, so the four strokes at the top, pointing left, must be *C*, and the next was *o* . . . He peered from his stone to the message on the birch rod. The *C* wasn't there. But the next feda was! And the two after that! He thrust his knuckle in his mouth and bit hard to stop himself crowing with excitement.

'Hey, what are you up to?'

Ket jumped with shock, and threw himself on top of his stone. But it was too late. Lorccán had already reached out to grab it.

'Don't!' cried Ket. 'That's mine!'

'Not now, it isn't!' Lorccán waved it in the air.

Blazing with fury, Ket launched himself at Lorccán. The other boy twisted and struggled, but Ket hung on, clawing at his arm, till the stone was back in his grasp. Triumphantly, he spun round and flung it towards the trees.

'There!' he panted. 'It's gone!'

'Ha, I can find it,' retorted Lorccán. He tried to step away, but Ket seized his léine. There was a loud ripping noise.

'Ket!' It was the shocked voice of Faelán. 'What is this rough behaviour?'

Ket dropped Lorccán's sleeve as if it were burning his hands and turned to face the druid.

'Young man, this is not the behaviour I expect from someone who aspires to be a druid.'

Ket's cheeks flared. From the corner of his eye, he saw Lorccán sidle towards the stone. He clenched his jaw.

'You have disappointed me,' the druid continued, shaking his head. Then he glanced up at the sky. 'Now, it is getting late . . .'

Lorccán stopped moving and all the fosterlings stared with dismay at the setting sun. Soon, the Spirits of the Dead would begin to stir.

Ket's eyes fell to the cairn. In the sunset, the rocks glowed pink.

'And they're not all rocks,' Ket remembered, his stomach twisting, 'some of them are skulls.'

He felt for the comfort of the red string at his wrist, and found nothing. He looked down. The string was gone. It must have been torn off when he struggled with Lorccán for the stone. He was gripped by a feeling of panic.

'I must start my vigil,' Faelán announced.

Tonight the druid would stand waiting and watching on the peak of the cairn, with the dead beneath him and firewood laid ready at his feet. Far off in Uisnech, when the Old Year ended, the leader of the druids would light the first spark to signal the New Year. Then a message of fire would spread across the land from peak to peak as every watching druid lit a flame.

'Who will carry my firewood up the cairn?' inquired Faelán.

'Not me,' whimpered Riona, backing away.

A taste of fear filled Ket's throat, but the druid's eyes came to rest on Bran.

'Bran, gather some wood and bring it up the mound for me,' said Faelán, and he strode across the Plain of Moytura towards the cairn.

Nessa hurried to Bran, her face creased with concern.

'Oh, Bran . . .'

'Pah!' Bran stuck out his chin and looked round defiantly. 'I'm not scared by ghost stories.' He picked up an armload of wood and marched off.

Nessa let out a sigh and turned to Ket.

'What were you and Lorccán squabbling about?' she asked.

'I—'

Before Ket could answer, Riona came bustling up like a herd dog scenting danger. 'Come on,' she urged, 'we have to get inside the tree!'

Nath-í's sleeve caught on the holly as they squeezed through the opening.

'Uch, this stuff scratches,' he complained.

'Careful, don't pull it down!' warned Nessa.

They all crowded in. Lorccán took the space in the middle and the others squashed around the edges, with bits of rotting tree trunk showering down on them. Ket could hear Riona breathing nervously beside him.

'Nath-í, when we were little, before you came, we always sneaked in here to sleep when it rained,' said Nessa.

'*I* never did,' said Lorccán.

It was true. Even when he was only seven, Lorccán had always slept outdoors beside the anruth.

'When I was little, I cried every night with home-sickness,' said Riona. 'Nessa, you used to comfort me, remember?'

'I remember,' said Nessa, 'and you made *me* cry.'

'And me,' said Ket.

'*I* never cried,' said Lorccán.

'I wish Bran would hurry up,' said Riona. 'It's nearly dark!' She leaned anxiously forward.

Peering through the slit in the trunk, they could all see Bran toiling up the cairn. He dropped the bundle of wood, and turned to scurry down again.

They heard the pounding of his feet, and the next moment he was scrambling through the entrance, gasping for breath.

'You made it just in time,' said Riona.

It was twilight now. As they watched, the colours of daylight bleached out of the world. The sky darkened. They could see the black shapes of the anruth huddled by the dead ashes of their fire, and the shadowy figure of the druid on the cairn. The last glow of sun, like a trickle of blood, stained the edge of the sky, and faded away. For a moment, the round, bright shape of a full moon hung above the treetops, then a bank of cloud drifted across, and they were left in darkness.

'The Spirits of the Dead are rising,' quavered Riona.

'Don't worry,' said Nessa reassuringly. 'They won't get past our holly.'

'The anruth don't have holly!' Riona protested.

'They could if they wanted,' said Nessa. 'They're not scared.'

Ket felt a tenseness in the group around him, then

suddenly Lorccán sprang to his feet.

'I'm not scared, either,' he exclaimed. 'I'm not skulking in here.'

Roughly, he pushed his way outside.

'Lorccán, don't! Come back,' wailed Riona.

There was no answer. They could hear his stumbling footsteps and then he disappeared in the darkness.

Inside the tree there was a stunned silence. Ket could feel the blood pounding in his ears. Far in the distance, there came an unearthly cry, followed by the sound of beating wings, growing steadily louder. Suddenly, thousands of black shapes came pouring into camp, whirling and diving. They churned up a wind that screamed and eddied about the tree. The fosterlings clung to each others' hands while the voices of the anruth rose in a rapid, nervous chant.

'Protect us!
Spirits of Earth, Sea and Sky
Protect us!
Spirits of Sun, Moon and Stars
Protect us!
Spirits of Fire, Water and Air
Remember our offerings
When the barrier
Between our worlds
Is rent asunder.
Take pity
In this time without time.

Take pity
Harm us not
Protect us
Till the New Year comes.'

The beating and flapping surged and ebbed, like a rolling wave.

Ket wanted to call to Lorccán, but no sound would come from his throat.

'Look!' breathed Nessa.

A tiny light was flickering in the blackness. As they watched, it grew larger until they could see it was a leaping fire on the top of the cairn. For a moment, the shape of the druid showed in front of it and then he disappeared.

There were murmurings and scrapings as they all strained forward to see what was happening.

'There he is! He's coming over here.'

A gleam was bobbing towards the camp. They let out a wavering cheer as Faelán, carrying the flame, appeared between the trees.

In front of the hollow oak, a sprawled figure lifted its head from the ground and rose slowly to its knees.

'Ah, Lorccán, so you do not fear the spirits,' said Faelán. 'Come; light the first fire for the New Year, and keep vigil with us for the night of Samhain.' He held out the torch, and Lorccán stepped forward.

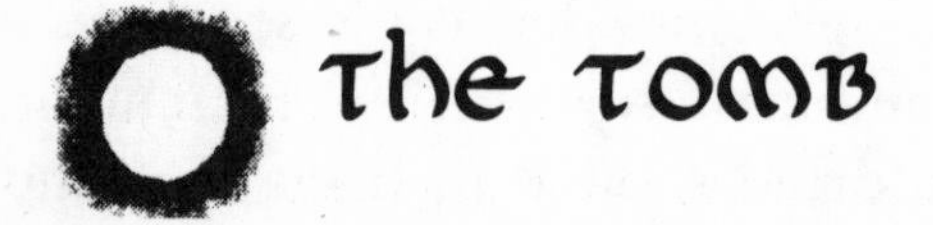

The Tomb

'Ooh, I don't know how Lorccán dared,' said Riona. '*I* couldn't go out there with all those spirits around!'

'Don't see how you could ever be a druid then,' said Bran.

'Weren't *you* scared climbing the mound of the Shadow Ones?' asked Riona. 'And walking on those skulls?'

'Well . . . I didn't look down,' admitted Bran.

'I wouldn't go near the dead tonight,' said Nath-í fervently.

Ket didn't want to either. But Bran had climbed the mound, and now Lorccán was out there with all the Spirits of the Dead roaming about . . .

With his insides turning to water, Ket forced himself to his feet.

'I'm going outside too.' He tried to sound brave as he thrust his way out of the tree. Rain pelted his face, and the air was so frosty it made him gasp.

'Ket, where are you going?' called Nessa anxiously.

The bright, welcoming circle of the campfire lay in front of him but Ket stared beyond it, across a world of darkness, to the small flicker of the Samhain fire high on the mound.

'To the cairn of the Shadow Ones,' he whispered.

As he passed the campfire, curious faces turned towards him. He saw Lorccán's astonished expression and the glint of Faelán's eyes. He was glad they couldn't see that his legs were as trembly as a newborn lamb's.

Rain ran down his hair and face as he stumbled forward. All around, in the murky night, shadows seemed to shift and quiver as if they were following him.

The grey mound of the cairn loomed in front. He could see the crest, lit by the dancing flames. And below . . . He jerked to a halt. There was the entrance to the tomb.

He stood in his wet clothes, teeth chattering, and stared at the low opening, half-sunk in the ground. What would he find in there? The Shadow Ones, or skeletons with bare, grinning skulls? He started to reach for the red band at his wrist, then remembered it was gone. Sweat joined the rain running down his forehead.

'Go on,' he growled at himself.

Step by unsteady step, he stumbled forward till he reached the cairn. Now he had to climb through that black hole into the earth. He took a shuddering breath, and lowered one foot. The next moment he was slipping and sliding on wet mud, and clutching at the massive stone doorposts. Then he was out of the rain, cowering inside a tunnel, with dry walls of stone curved around him. In the faint moonlight that came through the opening, he could see a paved floor sloping downwards.

Dragging his hands along the stonework, Ket took a few shuffling steps. Soon, his hands were patting air. It was dark in the depths of the tomb, but he sensed a chamber arching around him. He waited, ears straining, eyes trying to pierce the blackness. There were no sounds. No voices. No movements. All he could see was something glinting on the wall in front of him. As his eyes adjusted to the dark, a long, silvery shape emerged from the gloom. It seemed to be a horn, hanging by a string. Ket stretched out to touch it.

There was a dull *thud* and something landed on his foot. He glanced down. A large fleshy hand, the fingers half uncurled, was lying on his brogue.

Ket gasped and jerked his foot away. The hand thumped to the ground.

And now Ket saw an outflung arm in a long dark sleeve. He saw a body spattered with blood, and a pale, tallow-coloured face beneath a bronze helmet. Beside it was another body; and another – a whole grisly heap of them. He stared at their old-fashioned shields and broken swords. The Shadow Ones! The dead of Moytura!

He tried to back away, but his legs wouldn't move, and his arms, with a will of their own, reached for the horn. The string that held it disintegrated in a puff of dust, and the treasure dropped into his grasp. It gleamed with startling newness, as if it had just been made and polished.

And now, as though trapped in a dream, Ket lifted the instrument to his lips and blew. It gave a feeble squeak. He raised his head to take a deeper breath – and froze.

One of the dead warriors was looking straight at him.

'Is it time?' The man's voice was hollow and creaky.

Ket let out a terrified yelp, and dropped the horn. It clattered onto the stone floor as he turned and fled from the tomb.

Divination

'As if you really went inside,' scoffed Lorccán.

'Ket doesn't lie!' retorted Nessa loyally. 'You're just jealous.'

All the fosterlings were back inside the tree. Ket, wrapped tight in Nessa's cloak, was still shivering.

'Tell us what you saw, then,' said Lorccán.

Ket stared at him and tried to speak. Floating in front of his eyes were images of ghastly faces with flesh like raw white fat.

'Uh . . .' He shuddered and shook his head.

'See, you can't tell us,' said Lorccán.

Ket clenched his fists. If only he hadn't dropped the horn! If only he could have thrust that treasure all silver and gleaming under Lorccán's nose.

'Hey, listen,' said Riona.

From the tree above their heads came the chirrup of a wakening robin. The long night was drawing to an end.

The fosterlings crushed together in the entrance of the hollow oak and peered out. The flames of the campfire shot skywards as the anruth heaped on branch after branch.

'O Spirit of the Sun
Accept our offering of fire
Let a New Year dawn
O Spirit of the Sun,'

Faelán entreated.

Ket peered at the sky. Behind the flames there was nothing but blackness. The glare of the fire was so blinding, he could not even make out the grey shapes of trees or clouds. Then, with the cooing of a woodpigeon, came a faint glimmer of dawn. Ket let out a sigh.

'Maura,' said the druid, flourishing a strip of cloth, 'bind this about my eyes. It is time for the New Year divinations.'

Blindfolded, Faelán began to circle around the balefire. Ket watched with his heart in his mouth. Several times, the long feathered cloak almost swirled into the flames.

As the druid circled, he called on the spirits to guide him.

'Spirit of the Sea before me
Spirit of the Wind behind me
Spirit of the Sky above me
Spirit of the Earth beneath me.'

He halted, and tore the blindfold from his eyes.

'Stronger of sight than I
Reveal what befalls us!'

Everyone looked around expectantly, and then a redwing darted from a tree.

'A lucky omen!' cried Bronal.

Faelán smiled and nodded.

'Very soon we will hear good tidings,' he said.

All the anruth clamoured for a turn to wear the blindfold.

'First you must build the balefire higher,' said Faelán.

The anruth fed the flames, till the fire roared so high it dwarfed even the tall figure of Faelán. As its blasting heat spread to the tree where the fosterlings were huddled, Ket shrank away. He was filled with terror and awe, just as he'd been all those Samhains ago, when he'd seen the balefire for the first time. Just for a brief instant he was living that scene again. His father had brought him to the druid's camp and the little Ket was staring with fright at the flames, the crowds and lowing cattle. He remembered watching his father leave, longing to call out 'Stop!', to run after him and take his hand. But instead Ket had wrapped his arms around a tree, pressed his face into the rough bark, and willed himself to stand there with eyes clenched shut until his father was out of sight.

Now, as the sky lightened, there were mooings and the shuffle of feet among the trees. One by one, the people of the tuath, leading their cattle, emerged from the forest. The fosterlings peeked from the hollow oak, pointing with excitement at those they recognised. Ket's heart quivered when he saw his father. In memory, Ossian had been proud and tall, but here, draped in his dun brown cloak, he looked like a timid fieldmouse next to Morgor the Chieftain.

'Druid,' called Morgor, sliding a sparkling jewel from his finger, 'please accept another token of my appreciation.'

Everyone jostled to form a ring around the huge balefire. There were *shushes* and muffled curses as a few jittery cows pawed the ground and tried to back away. But at last they were all ready, waiting in a respectful hush.

'Let us discover the fate of the tuath for the coming year,' declared Faelán. He turned to the oldest anruth. 'Goll, you take the blindfold.'

Goll circled the flames, chanting just as the druid had done, and when he pulled off the blindfold a squirrel darted up a tree in front of him.

'An animal rising – good health,' cried Goll, sounding relieved.

Everybody cheered.

'Next.' Faelán nodded, and Goll handed the blindfold to Maura.

Bran began to giggle.

'She doesn't look much like a druid,' he said.

'She does so,' said Nessa.

Silently, Ket agreed with Bran. Maura had a figure like a bulging grey sack tied round the middle with string. As she bustled around the fire, she didn't look very majestic.

'Hey.' Lorccán jabbed Ket with his elbow. 'You're taking up too much room. I can't see.'

Angrily, Ket butted him back.

'You sillies, we don't have to stay in here anyway,' said Nessa. 'It's daylight now!'

She crawled out of the tree just as Maura pulled off her blindfold. There was a loud *hiss* from the anruth, and Maura looked aghast.

'A red-haired girl – ill fortune,' said Faelán sternly.

The crowd murmured angrily. Nessa stumbled to her feet, scarlet with embarrassment.

'Sorry!' she muttered.

'Oooh, Nessa,' said Riona, biting her finger. The fosterlings all hurried to Nessa's side.

'She didn't mean it,' said Ket.

'Do not despair!' cried Faelán, turning to the people of the tuath, 'You can yet invoke the good will of the spirits. To ensure the health and prosperity of your families for the coming year, cast your offerings on the sacrificial fire. Lead forth your beasts for saining.'

He beckoned to the fosterlings. 'Each of you take a branch of bog pine, and follow what the anruth do. This year, you can help with the saining.'

Trembling with excitement, Ket took his branch of pine and stepped forward. The heat was so intense he felt as if he was walking into the flames. He dabbed his torch at the balefire, and the ancient bog pine immediately blazed up in a bright white flare. Ket jumped back, terrified and exhilarated.

Morgor the Chieftain turned to the crowd, ostentatiously displaying a lime-coated shield with a shining boss. He cast it into the fire to gasps of approval and wonder.

'That boss looked like real gold,' said Lorccán in a hushed voice.

Morgor's herdboy was struggling to bring a fine brindled cow to the fire, but the creature dug in her hind legs, the bell around her neck making an agitated clanking noise.

'I'll make her come,' offered Lorccán, but before he could move, someone in the crowd gave the cow an impatient kick.

Next moment everyone was pressing forward, waving their offerings and clamouring with excitement. Ket found himself surrounded by a crush of surging bodies.

Carved wooden statues, broken swords, armbands, and dead chickens were flung over his head into the balefire. The stench of singed feathers and flesh mingled with the scent of burning pine wood as the towering flames devoured them all.

'Spirit of Fire, protect and purify!' The voice of the druid rose above the din.

There was laughter and shouting, lowings and bellowings as each reluctant cow, head tossing, eyes rolling, was prodded or dragged towards the flames.

Fleet-foot and nimble with happiness, Ket skipped between the crowds, his burning branch held aloft, circling and purifying the cows. He heard a howl behind him and turned to see a man being doused with a bucket of water, smoke billowing from his léine. Nath-í was backing away, his face white with dismay.

'Oooh, poor Nath-í must have set that man alight!' thought Ket.

Ossian beamed with pride when Ket circled his small, docile cow, the heat of the saining fire shimmering between them. Ket could see his father mouthing words, but couldn't hear his voice above the roar of the crowd. Then Ossian reached to pull a burning brand from the flames. Back in the ring-fort, the cold black hearth was waiting to be kindled by this spark from the New Year fire.

Gradually the crowd began to thin. As Ket watched the hindquarters of the last few cows sway out of sight between the trees, joy was bubbling out of him, like ale from an over-filled cup. At last, he'd played a part in the Samhain ceremony instead of standing aside watching and envying.

The anruth heaved the cauldron onto the sinking fire, and crowded close, eager to break their fast.

'Fosterlings!' Faelán's voice was hoarse. He waved a hand around the camp. 'Attend to this disorder.'

The six of them stood, sooty, dishevelled, toes bruised by trampling hoofs, hands smarting with burns, and gaped at the chaos. The monstrous balefire had scorched a wide black scar, and the ground around it was a churned-up mess of mud. Their bedding of heather branches was trampled everywhere, and fouled with steaming heaps of cow dung.

'Ooof, I can't, I'm too tired,' groaned Riona, plonking herself down.

'Riona, get up.' Nath-í tried to drag her to her feet, peering worriedly over his shoulder. 'Master Faelán says we have to tidy the mess.'

Nessa, quick and efficient as always, had already

fashioned a besom from a bunch of broken twigs and was beginning to sweep.

Lorccán's face took on a purposeful gleam. 'Bran,' he said, 'you pile all that soiled heather on the fire. Ket, you pick some fresh bedding. Nath-í, you find something to use for a shovel.'

Bran thrust his fists on his hips and glared at Lorccán. 'And what do you plan to do yourself?' he demanded.

But Ket was too keyed up to be bothered by Lorccán's bossiness. He had tasted what it was like to be part of the magic. Ripping up armloads of fresh heather, he raced hither and thither around the camp, all the while darting glances at Faelán. Was the druid watching him? Could Faelán see how keenly, how eagerly, Ket did his bidding?

If Ket had wanted to be a druid before, it was nothing to his longing now. He had to stay here. He *had* to!

spell words

The days sped by. Each night the moon rose later, and grew smaller and fainter, till finally it vanished completely and the nights of darkness came again.

On the last evening before the new moon, Ket was too strung-up to sleep. He wrapped his arms around his knees, and listened to the tune rippling from the druid's harp.

'Ket, this is the sleeping strain. Why have you not succumbed?' murmured Faelán.

Ket started, and glanced around him. Everyone else was deep in slumber.

'I . . .'

Hastily, he stretched out on the ground, but his

mind was seething. Why had the music failed to enchant him? What was wrong with him? He pressed his eyes shut and desperately tried to sleep.

'Ket?'

'Mmm?' Ket mumbled drowsily and opened one eye. It was still dark.

'Ket, it's the last day.' Nessa pulled the cover away from his chin. Immediately, the cold night air rushed in. He groaned and sat up, hugging the rawhide around him.

'It's not even dawn yet.' Casting his eyes upwards, he saw the sparkle of stars against the black sky, but no moon.

'Tonight it will be the new moon,' whispered Nessa. 'And I've been thinking. If Faelán sends me away . . .'

'He won't send you away!'

'If he does,' repeated Nessa firmly, 'then I want you to win.'

Ket reached out from his warm cover and took the hand she held towards him.

'And if he sends *me* away . . .' He stopped. There was a lump blocking his throat so that he could barely croak out the words. 'I want you to win.'

She squeezed his hand and lay down again. In a few moments he felt her fingers slacken as she drifted back to sleep.

Ket stayed sitting where he was, growing colder

and colder, as if all the blood was draining out of his body. From somewhere among the trees came the tentative trill of a robin. The figure of Faelán glided across the clearing, his arms raised, beginning to call up the sun.

Ket looked at him imploringly. 'Please don't send me away. *Please*!' he prayed.

Art and Bronal yawned noisily and rolled out of their covers to stoke up the fire. As the warm, yellow flames crackled into life, Ket straightened his stiff legs and stumbled to his feet.

Maura was propping lumps of dough against the three-pronged sticks in front of the fire, and the smell of toasting oatmeal filled the air.

Ket pulled a face. 'I'm too nervous to eat.'

'Me too!' Riona agreed.

Lorccán smiled and patted his belly. 'All the more for me, then.' And he stuffed the food in his mouth as if he had not a care in the world.

When the fosterlings gathered under the Sacred Yew for their morning instruction, Faelán regarded them solemnly.

'It is time to set you a more challenging task,' he said. Ket swallowed nervously. 'You have all shown competence at learning the tales, so now you can progress to the next level – the composition of poetry. This is a skill you will need in order to cast a spell.'

'Spells! We're going to learn magic!' said Riona.

'Here is a spell you might cast on a king or chieftain to improve the prosperity of his kingdom,' said Faelán.

'May the harvest of your fields be bountiful
May the harvest of your trees be bountiful
May the harvest of your rivers be bountiful—'

'But . . .'

The druid stopped reciting. 'Yes, Bran?'

The red-haired boy had screwed up his face. 'Fruit and crops don't grow in rivers,' he protested.

'Ah.' Faelán breathed a smile. 'I expected you to say that, Bran. The secret of the best poetry and the most potent magic is to use words that your listener has to interpret. It is not really fruit that grows in the rivers, but—'

'I know! It's *fish*!' said Lorccán. 'When you harvest a river, you catch fish!'

The druid nodded. 'Well done, Lorccán. Instead of using a simple word like *fish*, a poet says the *harvest of the river* or the *cattle of the sea.*'

'Cattle!' giggled Riona.

'And now, this is your task: I will give each of you a simple word and you will think of a poetic description. Bran, see what you can do with the word *snow*; Riona, your word is *hazelnut*; Lorccán, yours is *dead*; Ket, yours is *yew tree*; Nath-í, see what you can do with *the sun*; and Nessa . . . take the word *shield.* I will give you a few minutes to think of your answers.'

He leaned back and began to strum softly on his harp.

Ket was too nervous to think. Tonight it was the new moon. Tonight the druid was going to send one of them away. He had nearly failed the first test. If he failed now . . . He swung round to the Sacred Yew and pressed his hand against one of the three ancient trunks, pleading for help. He screwed his eyes shut, listening, feeling. At first, his senses were filled with useless, irritating noises: Riona's anxious breathing, Nessa's pacing, the twittering of chaffinches and tits in the branches over his head. Then gradually the sounds faded, and he felt as if he were sinking into the heart of the tree.

Faelán stopped strumming.

'Reveal your answers,' he said.

Ket blinked, as if he were rising out of sleep.

'I've got a good one!' said Lorccán. 'Can I go first?'

The druid inclined his head. 'Your word was *dead.*'

'Feast for crows!' said Lorccán, with relish.

'Ah, well done,' said Faelán.

Lorccán beamed with pride.

'I don't get it,' said Riona.

Nath-í made a face. 'You know, when there's a dead lamb, and the crows all come and feast on it,' he said.

'Eugh.'

'What did you think of for *hazelnut*, Riona?'

Riona looked proud. 'Cattle of the hazel tree!' she announced.

There was an uncomfortable silence, then Bran choked back a laugh.

The druid turned to him sternly. 'Bran? What is your description for *snow*?'

'White cloak,' said Bran.

'Ooh, that's good,' said Nessa.

'And Nessa, what is yours, for *shield*?' queried Faelán.

Ket saw Nessa ball her hands into tight fists.

'Protector of the heart?' she asked anxiously.

Faelán nodded. 'That will do.' He looked around. 'Anyone else?'

Ket took a deep breath. 'Me,' he whispered.

'Ah yes, what did you think of for *yew tree*?'

'Old One of the forest,' said Ket. To his annoyance, before Faelán could respond, Lorccán broke in.

'Nath-í,' Lorccán pointed. 'Nath-í hasn't done his yet.'

Ket bit his lip and turned. Had Nath-í managed to think up something for *sun*?

'The sun is a gleaming shield boss in the sky,' said Nath-í calmly.

Ket was startled. The druid stroked his beard.

'For your first attempt, you have all done well,' he said. 'This winter, when the king pays his visit to the chieftain, I think you fosterlings may accompany me as my retinue. You shall all compose poems of praise for the king.'

'The ones who are still here,' said Lorccán under his breath.

The First New Moon

'Will this day never end?' moaned Nessa. 'The suspense is killing me.'

'What are you so worried about?' said Riona. 'Master Faelán will never send *you* away.'

Nessa sighed. 'I wish I could see into the future.' She stripped some berries off a branch and trickled them through her fingers.

'Harvest of the yew tree,' murmured Nath-í, his eyes following the berries. 'If you were a druid,' he added, 'you could probably tell by the way those fall what's going to happen tonight.'

The fosterlings all stared at the small rosy fruit in Nessa's hand.

'Here, give them to me,' said Bran. He took the yew berries and tossed them into the air. One of them plopped into Lorccán's lap. 'Ooh look, Lorccán's going home tonight!'

Lorccán's face blanched with fury. He picked up the berry and flung it at Bran.

'It's not true!' he yelled. 'You just made that up!'

'Of course it's not true,' Bran scoffed. 'All divination is drivel.'

There was a shocked silence.

'But . . . but . . .' Riona stuttered.

'What do you mean?' growled Lorccán, crossing his arms.

Bran looked round at their startled faces.

'You're all so gullible,' he chortled.

He picked up a fallen feather and held it in the air. 'This is an omen!' he intoned, mimicking the druid.

Ket glanced over his shoulder, half hoping half fearing the druid would notice Bran's antics.

'I predict that a bird is going to fly past,' continued Bran.

He paused, and at that moment a fieldfare darted over their heads. He let out a snort at the expressions on their faces. 'Of course it came true,' Bran mocked. 'There are always birds flying around. Divination is just a trick.'

The others backed away from him, and glanced at each other.

'It's true if a real druid does it,' said Nessa firmly.

Shaking their branches of bells, the fosterlings marched to the fire, where Faelán and the anruth were waiting. The first pink of sunset was tingeing the sky as each took a rowan branch and cast it on the flames. Then, slowly, with Faelán leading the way, they circled the fire. Ket felt so proud he thought his head might start chiming like the bells.

'Spirit of the Moon
Arise from darkness.
Spirit of the Moon
Return and guide us,'

they chanted together.

The druid raised his arm and there, just where he pointed, Ket made out the faint, ghostly shape of the new moon. There were cheers around the fire. But while the anruth hoisted the cauldron on the flames, and tossed in herbs, laughing and chatting, the fosterlings drew together in a tight, nervous cluster.

'What do we do now?' whispered Nath-í.

They all looked at Faelán and saw that he was watching them. The anruth's babble died away, and they too turned to the druid. Ket could hear the tiny tinkle of the beads in Nessa's hair as she quivered beside him.

'Fosterlings,' Faelán's voice boomed out, 'your time of reckoning is upon you. Tonight I must choose the first of you to send away.'

Ket felt a tightening in his chest.

'The demands on a druid are arduous and challenging,' continued Faelán. 'Since the last new moon, I have observed that one of you does not have the strength to face those challenges . . .'

Ket felt as if someone was twisting his insides, wringing them till he couldn't breathe. The night he'd run away, too speechless and terrified to tell his part of the tale – was that what the druid meant? The tight feeling spread to his throat.

'It is not merely a matter of learning. As a druid, you must be able to lead others, to impress them with your power and ability.'

The druid paused. From the corner of his eye, Ket saw Lorccán lift his chin.

'However,' Faelán went on, 'though you cannot be a druid, I am sure you will make a fine wife and mother.'

Suddenly, Ket's legs were almost too wobbly to hold him up, but Nessa, standing beside him, went rigid, her gaze glued on Faelán.

Then the druid turned to the smaller girl, with the dark curls and the frightened eyes.

'Riona, I fear you do not have the strength to lead others, as a druid must. Your clan will find you a new foster home where you can learn to spin and weave, to dye cloth, brew ale and bake bread.'

Ket could see the utter relief in Nessa's body as she clasped an arm around the other girl.

Riona reached up to lay her fingers over Nessa's. 'You'll make a better druid than me,' she gulped.

'Now . . .' Faelán held out his hand. 'Your branch of bells.'

Ket felt as if his heart was being wrenched from his chest as Riona, with tears trickling down her cheeks, surrendered her branch.

'The rest of you,' said the druid, 'shall remain until the next new moon.'

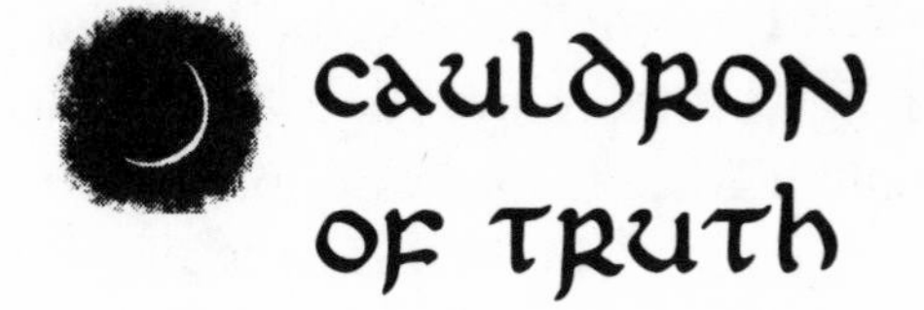

Cauldron of Truth

Next morning, Bran and Lorccán were restless and noisy, shouting and sparring with each other, while Ket, Nath-í and Nessa moped under the Sacred Yew.

'I wonder what Riona's feeling now,' said Ket.

'Ashamed and embarrassed,' muttered Nath-í.

Ket and Nessa glanced at each other. They both knew Nath-í was remembering his own feelings when he'd been cast off by a wood-turner for his clumsiness and sent to the druid's camp in disgrace.

'There's nothing to be ashamed about,' said Nessa

stoutly. 'Every person has to find the path that suits them. The druid's path just wasn't right for Riona. She thought she wanted to learn magic, but really she'll be much happier being a farmer's wife, doing cooking and spinning and all that womanly stuff.'

'Would you prefer that too, Nessa?' asked Nath-í.

'Me?! Can you see me standing at a loom and weaving all day? Or cooking? I hate cooking! I don't mind hunting for game, but someone else can cope with the feather-plucking and pot-stirring, thank you very much. No, I'd much rather be a druid.' There was a moment's uncomfortable silence, and she flushed. 'That's if Master Faelán chooses me,' she added. 'But of course, he'll probably choose one of you.'

Nath-í shook his head gloomily. 'He won't be choosing me. I always fail at everything.'

Ket felt sick. He hated wishing that his friends would be sent away so that he could win.

Bran and Lorccán rolled to the ground, punching and yelling, just as Faelán appeared in the clearing.

'Maura,' called Faelán, 'these twigs are in need of some exercise. Time for a session of weapon-training.'

'*Weapon-training*?' squeaked Nath-í. 'But . . . but . . . I thought we wouldn't need that any more.'

The look of dismay on his face was so comical, they all burst out laughing.

'Young man, I would be failing as your foster father if I neglected your training in arms,' Faelán replied. 'Only one of you is destined to be a druid, and even he, or she, should have a knowledge of weapons. Maura, are you ready?'

Maura was balancing an apple on top of a pole.

'Oh no, we don't have to try to hit that, do we?' moaned Nath-í, as Maura headed purposefully towards them, slingshots swinging from her hand.

'I'll show you how to do it,' said Lorccán, already casting around for a suitable stone. But as he straightened up, weighing one in his hand, Nath-í pointed.

'Look!' His face lit up with relief. 'Visitors!'

Sure enough, through the gap in the trees, they could see a procession of people crossing the plain.

'They're from your clan, Nessa,' exclaimed Ket.

In front plodded the lawgiver, Brehon Áengus, face shining, belly bulging, and the gold Collar of Truth gleaming around his short neck.

'Fáilte,' he called. 'Good health to you.'

'Good health to you,' replied the druid.

The visitors halted.

'Welcome to the Sacred Yew,' said Faelán.

'We bring offerings.'

Brehon Áengus was puffing as he bowed over his fat belly. Two young boys staggered out of the crowd, balancing a basket between them. They laid it down and the fosterlings' eyes widened in rapture. They could see the yellow rind of a hard cheese, the crust of a loaf, and a fresh, bloody haunch of oxflesh.

'We'll eat well tonight,' whispered Bran.

'Druid of the Forest,' said the brehon, 'the clan of Ardal are come to ask the spirits for guidance in settling a dispute.'

'What is your dispute?' queried Faelán.

'Well, this farmer here . . .' Brehon Áengus indicated the man beside him.

'Uncle Tirech!' breathed Nessa.

'Tirech,' continued the lawgiver, 'makes a claim against Gortigern.'

Nessa gave a little gasp.

'He claims that Gortigern entered his house without permission—'

'You liar!' A huge, brawny man thrust his nose into Tirech's face. 'You invited me.'

'Invited you?!' Tirech's voice rose to a squeak. 'Not likely.' He shook his fist under Gortigern's nose. 'You insult my wife, you kick my dogs, you knock over my lamps, you deliberately leave my gates open so my animals wander out. You . . . you . . .'

Gortigern burst out laughing. 'You snivelling weakling,' he jeered.

Tirech's face grew purple, and he ripped his sword from its scabbard.

'Show him, Tirech!' yelled a voice, but the druid stepped between them.

'Enough,' he said.

'Oof!' Nessa stamped her foot in frustration. 'Gortigern deserves it,' she growled. 'He bullies everyone!'

'Gortigern of the clan of Ardal,' said Faelán sternly, 'do you deny the charge?'

'Pah,' snorted Gortigern.

The druid turned to Tirech. 'Tirech of the clan of Ardal, are you prepared to submit your claim to the Cauldron of Truth, and abide by the decision of the spirits?'

Tirech thrust his sword into its sheath and nodded.

'Very well, we shall prepare the Cauldron of Truth,' said Faelán. He turned to the fosterlings. 'Nath-í and Ket . . .' Ket started with surprise. 'Bring me the water from the Sacred Spring.' Faelán gestured to the ox horn, traced in silver, suspended from the branches of the yew. Every morning he took the vessel and refilled it in a secret ceremony at the Sacred Spring deep in the forest.

Ket grabbed Nath-í by the sleeve before he could move. '*I'll* carry it,' he whispered. 'You might spill it!'

Conscious of everyone watching, he reached into the tree and closed his hands around the smooth, yellowed horn. He lowered it slowly, careful not to let it brim over. With firm, proud steps, he moved towards the cauldron, tilted the vessel and let the water trickle in. There was a lull as everyone waited for it to heat and simmer, and then, to his astonishment, Nath-í began to chant.

'Spirit of the Water
Spirit of the Fire
When the lots are cast
Reveal who is the liar.'

The song ended, and Ket backed towards the yew.

'Hey, Nath-í, that was really clever,' whispered Nessa. 'Did you make that up?'

Nath-í grinned. 'Was it all right?'

Ket looked at his friend's glowing face, then at Faelán nodding approval, and a dismal, sinking feeling sucked at his stomach. This task had been a chance to prove his worth, and all he had done was carry water. While Nath-í – fumble-fingers Nath-í – had composed a poem, and cloaked himself in glory.

As Ket struggled to look delighted and admiring like everyone else, Bran slid up beside him. Ket braced himself for a jeering remark.

'How can you smile like that?' demanded Bran under his breath. 'If I was you, I'd want to clout him.'

Ket was dumbfounded. Bran was offering sympathy instead of scorn.

'It's my own fault,' muttered Ket. 'I should have let him carry the water.'

'If you'd let him carry the water, he would have

spilt it!' protested Bran. 'You stopped him making a fool of himself and now look, everyone's fawning over him instead! That's not fair.'

Ket sent his surprising ally a glance of gratitude, then they both turned to watch as the druid opened the pouch at his belt and rummaged inside.

Faelán drew out two carved birch rods and lifted them into the air.

The five fosterlings looked at each other.

'It's ogham!' hissed Lorccán.

'These lots represent Gortigern the defendant and Tirech the accuser.' The druid crossed to the fire and held the rods above the steaming water. He looked sternly at the two men. 'I shall cast them into the Cauldron of Truth. If your lot floats on the surface, you are speaking truth. If it sinks, then you are guilty of lying.'

The lots landed with a splash, and everyone crowded forward. Ket stretched on his toes and craned his neck, trying to see what was happening.

'They're both floating,' said a disappointed voice.

'Ha,' said Gortigern.

At that moment the water bubbled more violently, and one of the rods tilted and began to sink. The crowd rumbled with excitement.

'Which one is it? Which one?'

Faelán leaned over the cauldron and plunged his arm into the boiling water. With no sign of pain, he stepped back, holding the lot aloft so everyone could see.

'Gortigern mac Ardal,' he boomed.

Gortigern glowered and crossed his arms.

Ket stared at the black strokes then glanced round eagerly for Nessa, but she was gone, wriggling through the crowd to Tirech's elbow. Ket closed his eyes, burning the shape of the feda into his memory.

'It must be *G*,' he thought, '*G* for Gortigern! And the other is *T* for Tirech.'

Brehon Áengus clapped his hands. 'Gortigern mac Ardal, I pronounce you guilty. If this judgement be false, may the Collar of Truth tighten and choke me!'

There was a quivering, expectant pause. Everyone pressed closer, trying to see the gold torque around his neck. Ket felt a sharp elbow in his ribs, and someone's noisy breathing filled his ear. The brehon waited, his arms spread out dramatically, then Faelán's voice broke the silence.

'The spirits have spoken,' he cried. 'The judgement is made and proven.'

Excited murmurs rippled through the crowd.

The lawgiver held up his hand. 'The penalty for entering a dwelling without permission is a fine of one heifer-calf.'

'Gortigern, step forth to accept your penalty,' ordered Faelán.

The press of bodies shifted to make way for the glowering Gortigern, but Ket had seen enough. He wormed his way out of the crush and burst free, his eyes flying to the Sacred Yew. Lorccán and Bran were there already, crouched beside the ogham rod. When they saw him coming, they ran off laughing.

Nath-í sat in a forlorn huddle a short distance away.

'I didn't see,' he moaned. 'I got pushed out of the way, and those two won't tell me anything.' His eyes flicked in the direction Lorccán and Bran had taken.

Ket looked into the doleful face and sighed resignedly. How could he refuse to tell?

'Wasn't that exciting!?' cried Nessa, running to join them. 'When Brehon Áengus called out that challenge about the Collar of Truth, I almost died. What if it had really tightened and choked him? Imagine having a magic neck torque like that!' Her eyes were as sparkly as the gold beads in her hair. 'Do you think Gortigern will pay his fine? I bet he refuses. And then what will happen?' She twisted round to watch her clan march off down the path. 'Oh, I *wish* I could go home with them and see!'

Ket stared at her in astonishment.

'Aren't you interested in the ogham?' he asked. 'We found out two more.'

'The ogham!' Nessa swung back towards him. 'I nearly forgot. Let's look at the message.'

As they crouched by the rod, Nath-í leaned over their shoulders.

'Look!' Ket exclaimed. 'The second feda – it's the *T* from Tirech. That means the first word starts with *h-t* . . .' He stopped, bewildered.

'That's silly,' said Nessa. 'There isn't any word that starts with *h-t*.'

'There must be. Wait, if we put in the other feda . . . We don't know the one with three flat strokes, but then . . .' He sounded out each feda as he pointed. 'There's *m-n-o*. And the second word is *r-o* . . .' His voice trailed away.

'*Ro* isn't a word either.'

They glared at the ogham rod.

Nath-í brushed back his long fringe and peered earnestly at the markings.

'I don't get how you worked out any of it,' he muttered. 'How did you get *ro*? And *ht*?'

Nessa threw up her hands in exasperation 'It doesn't matter. They're not right anyway. We must have made a mistake.'

As Ket slumped back on his heels, Lorccán came sauntering over.

'Well,' he grinned. 'Bet you can't work it out. Bet I read the message first.'

Fians

The Spirit of the Sun was weakening. Every day the hours of light grew shorter. Ket watched the druid anxiously as he scanned the skies. Surely soon Faelán would call for the ceremony of Midwinter to coax back the departing sun. Hunger loomed over the druid's camp. The offerings of oxflesh, cheese and bread were long gone. There were no more apples on the trees and the birds had eaten the last of the blackberries.

'What are you all lolling about for?' Maura demanded. 'Take your slingshots and go find something for the pot, or we'll all be eating boiled water for dinner.'

'Take care!' warned Goll, when he saw the fosterlings headed for the forest. 'I hear the fians are about.'

'Hey, I want to see them!' yelled Lorccán, sprinting forward.

Nath-í faltered.

'Maybe we shouldn't go in then,' he said.

'They're not stopping me looking for my dinner,' said Nessa, not slowing her stride.

Ket halted next to Nath-í.

'Do you think they'll attack us?' asked Nath-í.

'We don't have anything to steal,' said Ket.

They both hesitated, remembering stories they'd heard of the wild young outlaws who roamed the forests, thieving and raiding.

'Scared, little minnows?' jeered Bran from the edge of the trees.

'No,' snapped Ket. 'We're coming.'

As soon as they entered the forest, Nath-í crouched down and began to poke among the fallen leaves. 'I think I'll just look for nuts,' he said.

'I don't want acorns for dinner again,' said Ket crossly. 'Where are the others? Why didn't they wait?' He paused, listening, but all he could hear was the gentle gurgle of the river. He started through the trees, calling their names. 'Nessa? Bran? Lorccán?'

A crow flew upwards with a screech of alarm, 'Gaug! Gaug!'

Dense thickets of gorse and blackthorn flanked the path, and overhead, the bare, wintry branches of oaks and hazel trees curled like claws.

Ket looked round for something to eat. Maybe he could find a few leaves of chickweed. Even the bitter sloes of the blackthorn would be better than nothing. He followed the eager *chat chat* of a fieldfare, hoping she had found a last bunch of blackberries they could share. But he found her pecking at bright red holly berries, and shook his head in disappointment.

'Those you can keep for yourself,' he muttered.

From beyond the bushes, came the thud of hoofs, and then the whinny of a horse. Ket jerked round in panic. Only chieftains and fians rode horses. He began to run, but a stallion burst out of the trees, rearing and crashing, and blocked his path. The rider was a boy not much older than Ket, with gleaming eyes in a filthy face.

'Hand over your silver,' he demanded.

'I . . . I don't have any,' stammered Ket.

The boy hooted.

'This fine young lord claims to have nothing!' he shouted.

Ket heard other fians whistling and jeering among the trees.

The boy slid from his mount and sauntered forward. Hot animal scent emanated from the strips of untanned, bloody fur he wore as clothes. 'What's that, then?' he demanded, thrusting a finger at Ket's cloak pin. 'Give it.'

Ket felt a surge of fury. He lifted his knee and aimed a kick right into the boy's stomach.

'Ooof!'

The young fian reeled back, his eyes wide with astonishment.

Ket whirled round, looking for a way to escape. There were shouts from the other riders, and he could hear their horses crashing towards him. Another horse lunged out of the trees.

Ket dived at the river. He gasped as he hit the cold water, and sank. His feet touched bottom, and he burst up, gulping for air, his long wet hair streaming over his face. A horse leapt in after him as he plunged for the opposite bank. He was slithering and scrambling up the side when a whip *thwacked* the ground beside him, and mud shot into his eyes. He hurtled forward, threw himself under a gorse bush, and burrowed among the branches, ignoring the spikes clawing at his clothes.

'Spirit of the Gorse,' he panted, 'hide me, protect me!'

He hunched there, soaked and shivering, and, just for a moment, above the noise of the fians' angry thrashing, he thought he heard the tinkle of bells.

One of the outlaws heard it too.

'Hey, listen.'

'It's the druids. They're coming.'

'They'll cast a spell on us.'

'I'm leaving.'

There were a few scuffles and grunts, a stifled whinny, and then the thud of hoofbeats fading into the distance.

The ringing of bells grew louder and Ket crawled from his hiding place just as Goll and the other anruth marched into view on the far bank.

'Ket, are you all right?' Nath-í burst out of the group. 'I saw the fians attacking you and I ran for help!' He skidded on the muddy slope and Goll grabbed him by the tunic.

'Hey, Ket!' The anruth pointed to a dead birch tree fallen across the water. 'You don't have to swim back, you can cross there,' he called.

Ket edged his way along the slippery trunk, his teeth chattering with cold. 'Th-they ran when they heard your bells,' he stammered.

As he reached the other side, Bran, Nessa and Lorccán bounded out of the trees. Nessa's face shone with triumph. She was twirling her slingshot and dangling two dead hares across her shoulder.

At the sight of Ket's bedraggled figure, the three hunters stopped short.

'What happened to you?!'

'The fians,' said Nath-í, 'they—'

'Oh Ket, did they hurt you?' cried Nessa.

Ket felt more pathetic than a wet feather. His cheeks flamed.

'Where'd they go?' demanded Lorccán, scanning the forest in frustration.

'They'll be far on their way now,' said Goll.

'If I'd been here, I would have shown 'em!' Lorccán dropped his slingshot and began to punch an imaginary opponent.

'I did show them!' said Ket. 'I—'

Lorccán spun round and made a feint at his jaw. Ket blocked it and skipped backwards.

'Hey!' squawked Nath-í as Ket stepped on his toe.

'Enough horsing around,' said Goll. 'Lorccán, did you catch something for our dinner?'

'Huh.' Lorccán snatched up his weapon. 'I saw this really big juicy badger, and I would have got it, only Nessa was hogging all the good stones.'

There was a spluttered exclamation from Nessa.

'I found some hazelnuts,' said Nath-í.

'Anyway, I bet the fians don't hunt with silly old slingshots,' said Lorccán. 'I bet they have big long spears. And bows and arrows. If I was a fian I'd have a spear as long as that tree, with five spikes on it. And I could kill anything.' He snapped a branch off the fallen birch, and as they headed back to camp he whipped every bush and fern that grew along the path.

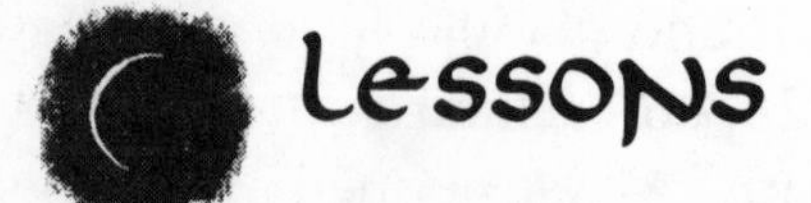

Lessons

It was three days until the next new moon. The camp lay sodden under winter rain. The fire was reduced to a pile of smouldering wood, where only a few embers glowed under the shelter of the cauldron.

The fosterlings, waiting for their morning lesson, huddled beneath the dense, spreading branches of the Sacred Yew. They were bundled in every scrap of fur they possessed and their breaths hung in the air in white clouds.

Nath-í wiped his streaming nose with his sleeve.

'I've thought of a poem,' he snuffled. The others turned to him in surprise. 'See if you can guess who it's about.'

'Fleetest of foot
Bravest and bold
Keenest of mind
When tales are told . . .'

Ket saw Lorccán draw himself up expectantly.

'Hair of fire
With beads of gold!'

Nath-í finished.

'It's Nessa!' cried Ket.

Lorccán tossed his head.

'Nath-í, thank you!' Nessa's cheeks were flushed, her eyes sparkling. Ket wished he'd been the one to compose a poem for her.

'Hey, listen to this one!' Lorccán flung back his fox-fur cloak and took up a stance, arms flexed. His fair hair shone, and the raindrops on his cape glittered like jewels.

'Muscles so strong
And hair so long.'

He thumped himself on the chest. 'How's that?'

'You're not supposed to make up poems about yourself,' said Ket.

Bran jumped to his feet.

'Here's another stanza.' He copied Lorccán's pose.

'Writer of
The worst song!'

He squealed and ducked as Lorccán aimed a blow at his shoulder.

Nath-í chuckled, then doubled over with a hacking cough. Nessa rubbed his back anxiously.

'Nath-í isn't tough enough to be a druid,' said Lorccán. 'Look at me!'

He strutted into the rain and held out his arms, tilting his face to the sky.

'Ah, Lorccán, I am pleased to see you participating in the Greater Harmony,' said Faelán.

Ket, swinging round, realised that Lorccán had spied the druid approaching. The druid's eyes were grey as the clouds, his hair and beard dripping with rainwater. The feathered cloak was spiky and bedraggled.

Abashed, the other fosterlings shuffled out from the shelter of the tree.

'Feel the elements,' cried Faelán.

'I feel them all right,' muttered Bran in Ket's ear. 'They're cold and wet.'

'Master Faelán,' said Nessa. 'I think Nath-í needs one of your cures.'

Faelán turned his attention to Nath-í, who was holding his chest and struggling to breathe. 'You must place an oak log on the fire to draw off your illness. While to soothe your cough, grind some hazelnuts and mix them with nectar from those blooms . . .' The druid gestured to the hollow oak. Shining like a crown in the winter gloom, a cluster of greenish-white flowers sprang from the ivy that clambered over the bare branches. 'Now, how about the rest of you? What did you observe, skulking there under the trees? Have you learnt anything about the Greater Harmony?'

Lorccán looked smug while the others glanced at each other.

'Uuh . . . the leaves have fallen off some of the trees,' said Nessa, 'that oak tree, and the birches, and the aspen . . .' Her voice tailed away and there was a pause.

'And what else?'

'Some of the birds have gone away,' offered Ket.

'But now there are different ones,' Lorccán burst in. 'I saw the wild geese arriving. I saw them first, before anyone else!'

'And you tried to get one with your slingshot, and missed,' hooted Bran.

'Bran, I have told you before, we do not point out others' errors or failings unless it is necessary,' admonished the druid. 'Have you a useful contribution to make? What changes have you observed?'

'I've seen fieldfares, and redwings about.'

'That is so,' said the druid, 'but what else has changed, apart from the birds and the leaves? Nath-í, what have you observed?'

Nath-í bit his lip and looked baffled. 'It's got colder!' he blurted out at last.

This time, they all started to giggle, until the druid held up a finger.

'That is not to be scoffed at,' he said. 'Never take the weather for granted. An oddity out of season – a warm night in winter, or a frost in summer – is a message from the spirits. An omen. If you become a druid, if you want to foretell the future . . .' His voice grew deep and solemn. 'You must be alert for omens.'

Behind the druid's back, Bran crossed his eyes and pretended to tug solemnly at an imaginary beard. Hurriedly, Ket averted his gaze. The druid was pointing at two fieldfares squabbling over holly berries.

'Those tiny birds have travelled over the sea from far-off lands,' he said. 'Every year they fly here, knowing that in our forest they will find berries to sustain them through the winter. If a tiny creature like a fieldfare can detect and use the pattern of the seasons, so can you.' He looked down again. A spider was crawling up his robe, spindly legs wavering and wobbling. When it was halfway up, Faelán coaxed it onto his finger, and gently transferred it to the trunk of the Sacred Yew. 'So . . .' He looked around at the upturned faces of the fosterlings. 'You must learn the pattern, the natural order of all things, in such intimate detail that you will recognise the unusual – the omens. Then, if you are chosen to be an anruth, I will teach you what those omens mean.'

They watched Faelán glide away, to vanish into the mist.

'You're right, Ket,' murmured Nessa. 'He doesn't make any sound when he walks.'

She took a few steps, trying to copy, but her rawhide brogues rustled the leaves, and a twig broke with a loud *snap.* 'It's impossible!' she said. 'Only a druid can do it.'

'Huh, it's just 'cause he has bare feet,' said Bran. 'Anyone could do it without these big flapping things on their feet.'

'Big flapping things!' Nessa protested. 'I spent hours sewing those pelts into brogues for you!'

'Bran,' said Ket, 'if you don't believe the druid has special powers, what are you doing here? Why do you put up with all this?' He gestured at the thick pall of mist, and the huddle of wet, cold figures with rain trickling down their faces. 'You could be living in a proper house somewhere, and sleeping in a real bed.'

Bran snorted. 'You think you can trick me into leaving.' His tone was scornful. 'Well, I'm staying right here. I want to be the one who tells people what to do just as much as you do.' Ket opened his mouth to object but Bran went on speaking. 'Anyway, when I'm a druid, I'm going to build myself a palace like a king. People will come *there* to bring offerings and worship, not to some mouldy old tree.'

'But . . . but . . . you *have* to live with the trees and the creatures, and sleep under the stars. You have to be part of the Greater Harmony, otherwise you won't see the changes, the omens . . .' Nessa's voice faltered and her forehead puckered worriedly.

Bran laughed. 'You really believe that stuff, don't you? Well, don't worry. I'll learn all the right moves from old Feather-cloak. No one will even dare to *breathe* unless I tell them to. I can wave my arms around and scrape ogham on bits of wood as well as anyone. Only *I'm* going to do it in comfort!'

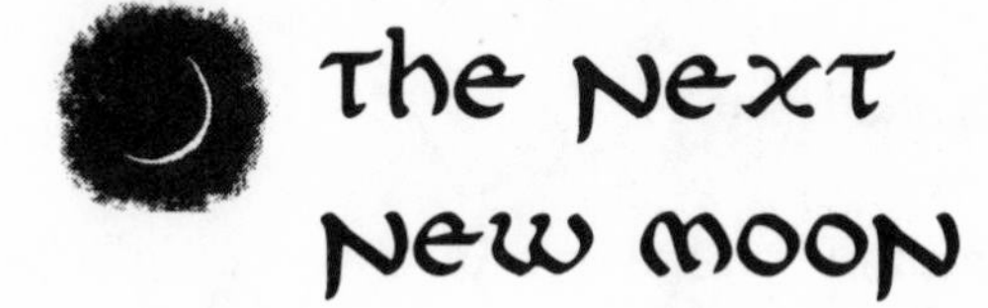

The Next New Moon

'Nessa, do you think Bran's right? Do you think everything Faelán does is just pretence?'

Nessa stabbed with her bone needle, yanked angrily on the rawhide thread for two more stitches, then tied a knot.

'There.' She tossed the mended brogue to Nath-í and turned to Ket. 'Of course not!' she snapped. 'You told me yourself how he cast a spell on your father. And he worked out that Gortigern was lying. You saw him use the ogham sticks, and plunge his arm into boiling water.' She stood up, brushing dead leaves from her skirt, and flounced off.

'Ow!' Nath-í hastily drew his foot out of the brogue. 'Nessa, you left the needle in!' But Nessa was gone.

The camp simmered with unease, for tonight it was the new moon again, and one more of them would be sent away. Even Nessa was grumpy.

'Here, Nath-í.' Ket tugged off his own shoes. 'Take mine. I want to try going barefoot like Faelán and the anruth.'

'You'll freeze,' said Nath-í.

'They manage.'

Ket took a tentative step, trying to be as light as possible. Putting his weight on a heel first, he was rolling very carefully onto his toe, when he sensed eyes watching. He turned to catch Lorccán grinning at him. Burning with embarrassment, Ket scurried from the camp. He sped past the cairn of the Shadow Ones, haunted by the memory of dead, white faces, and only slowed his pace when he reached the far side of the plain. Here, masked by mist and drizzle, he tried again.

Casting a glance over his shoulder, he began to tread cautiously, tilting forward, straining intently to hear his own footfalls.

A hare was propped on its haunches in the long heather ahead of him. Step by cautious step, Ket crept towards it. He could see the whiskers on its twitching nose, and the black hairs on the tips of its ears. He was nearly close enough to touch it before the creature bounded away.

Elated, Ket straightened up and saw Faelán heading up the hill from the bog. 'Did you see?' Ket called out in excitement. 'Did you see how close I got to that hare?'

The druid smiled and stooped to remove a tiny wisp of feather down caught on a leaf. As he spoke, he stroked it gently with his fingers.

'So, you are studying the natural order. What else do you observe?'

Ket felt a rush of anger and disappointment. Would he never win the druid's praise?

Somewhere to his right, a bird let out a trill, and in the distance another answered.

'Those are wrens!' said Ket, proud he could recognise their call.

'Good. And what are they saying?'

Saying? What are they *saying*? Ket gaped at Faelán in disbelief.

The druid cocked his head, listening. 'They are sending each other messages of alarm,' he said. 'You must have frightened them. Try to move more surreptitiously.'

Ket stared after his retreating back, feeling deflated.

Now, when he tried to move, he could only stumble. Every muscle in his back and legs was tight, and his feet were numb and clumsy.

The fosterlings poked morosely beneath the dripping trees, seeking out rowan boughs for the evening ceremony. The clouds hung low, spreading through the forest and matching their mood. The only sounds in the muffling greyness were the occasional snap of a twig or a subdued murmur. Ket, taking hold of a fallen branch, felt someone tugging the other end.

'This one's mine!' hissed Lorccán. 'I found it first.'

When the fosterlings trailed back to camp, Maura surveyed them, hands on hips. 'What a gloomy bunch you are!' she scolded. 'Well, I've got something to stir you up. Master Faelán says you're to have a lesson in spear-throwing.'

'Spear-throwing!' cried Lorccán, tossing down his rowan branch.

'Oh no,' moaned Nath-í.

'Your target's over there.' Maura pointed at a rotting tree stump.

'Can I go first?' asked Lorccán.

'All right, there you are.'

She handed Lorccán a stick with a pointed stone tied to one end.

'This isn't a real spear,' he objected.

'It's fine to learn with,' said Maura. 'Now, watch how to throw it.'

Her own spear had a long ash handle and a gleaming bronze head. She took a few bouncing leaps on the balls of her feet, balanced, and let fly. The spear made a whirring sound, then crunched into the heart of the target.

'Easy! I can do that!' said Lorccán. He thumped forward and flung his stick, but instead of flying through the air, it twanged into the ground at his toes, spattering him with mud. He stared down in surprise. 'Stupid stick!' he exclaimed.

'You didn't hold it right,' said Maura. 'Rest it in your fingers like this.' She held out her hand to show them. 'That's right, Nessa. You have a go.'

Plaits swinging, Nessa ran forward. She stopped, adjusted her stance, and hurled the stick. It thudded into the base of the trunk.

'Yes!' cheered Ket.

'Well done,' said Maura. 'Now, Nath-í, how about you?'

Nath-í backed away, stumbling over his own feet.

'If I try, it'll probably fly in the wrong direction and kill someone,' he said.

'You can't hurt anyone with that spear,' said Lorccán. 'Go on, try.'

The fosterlings forgot the rain, the cold and their

looming fate. They raced backwards and forwards, hurling the spear, shouting encouragement and laughing at each other. The tree stump grew more and more splintered as everyone's aim improved. At last, even Nath-í managed to hit it, though when he shouted in triumph and pulled the spear from its target, the stone tip snapped off the end.

'I've broken it!' said Nath-í ruefully.

Lorccán spun round to Maura.

'Can we use the real spear now?' he demanded.

Maura, picking up the damaged one, shook her head. 'Not now,' she said. 'Look.'

They followed the direction of her gaze and saw Faelán and the anruth gathering by the fire. The day was ended and it was time for the new moon ceremony. Instantly, the joy and excited banter were snuffed out. 'Come on,' said Maura.

In sober silence, the fosterlings followed her across the clearing.

Dense clouds still covered the sky. Faelán, lifting his arm to chant, added an extra plea.

'Spirit of the Moon
Hid from our sight
Arise from darkness
And pity our plight.
Spirit of the Moon
Return and guide us.'

Everyone peered up anxiously, hoping for a break in the clouds. Ket blinked as raindrops spattered into his eyes, but, if the moon was there, it remained hidden.

The druid fingered his beard. 'Art,' he said, in a slow, meditative way, 'fetch me a branch of broom.'

The anruth hurried across the clearing, and his footsteps faded away as he was swallowed up by the forest. The fosterlings drew together, silent and watchful. Darkness crept over them.

At last there came a rustling among the trees. A figure moved in the murk and a moment later, Art burst into the firelight brandishing a long, bushy branch.

'Ah.' Faelán grasped it and raised it above his head. 'Spirits of the Air, dispel these clouds and let us see your guiding light!' he commanded. He turned, sweeping the air with the branch.

Ket felt a puff of wind dance around his legs and curl the hem of his léine. The flames in the fire flickered and crackled. A murmur started in the woods and rose to a howl then the next moment a gale came tearing through the camp. Ket's arm flew to shield his eyes as spiky bits of leaf and twig blew into his face.

'Calm, be calm.' The tall figure of the druid loomed up beside the fire. 'Hear me, Spirits of the Air and cease your fury!' With a sharp movement, he cast the branch of broom onto the fire. 'Burn! Burn! Consume all anger!'

For a moment longer the spirits raged, and then,

as fast as they had come, they faded away. Cautiously, Ket lowered his arm. The air felt as if it was holding its breath.

All eyes turned to the sky. The clouds had been swept away and there, shining and clear, was the new moon.

The anruth and the fosterlings cheered. Laughing and chattering, they scrambled for their places around the fire.

Gratefully, Ket sat down and thrust his frozen feet towards the flames. Immediately, he let out a squawk, and jerked them back. It felt as if his toes were on fire.

'Hey, what have you been up to?' said Goll. 'Where are your brogues?'

'I took them off.' Ket gulped, trying not to cry. 'Druids don't wear shoes. *You* don't wear shoes.'

Goll chuckled. 'Yes, but I didn't start by leaving them off in the middle of winter. You'll get chilblains. Here, give us a look.' He pried Ket's hands away and tutted at the red, throbbing toes. 'Wrap them up now, and don't put them too close to the fire.' He tucked a corner of his squirrel-fur cloak around Ket's feet. 'In the morning I'll make you a poultice of mullein leaves.'

Faelán lifted his finger for attention, and Ket glanced worriedly at Goll.

'If I'm still here in the morning,' he muttered.

'I'm sure you'll be fine.' Goll patted his shoulder.

All eyes turned to the druid as he began to speak. 'Tonight is the second new moon, and once again, one of you fosterlings must be sent away.' There was no sound in the camp. Even the fire seemed to have ceased its crackling. He looked at the five tense figures in front of him. 'Lorccán . . .' he said.

Lorccán?! The blood pounded in Ket's head. 'You have shown you are a strong, confident leader,' Faelán continued, nodding approval and Ket felt a flood of disappointment. 'And Nessa, you are a highly capable and reliable young lady. As for Nath-í . . .' The druid shook his head, but he was smiling at the same time. 'Nath-í, I am impressed by your skill with words,' said Faelán.

Ket clenched his hands. His palms were sweaty. There was only himself and Bran left. He held his breath as the druid spoke the next name.

'Bran . . .' he said.

Ket felt the air *whoosh* from his lungs. He was the last! He was . . . A roaring filled his ears, almost blocking out Faelán's voice. He was vaguely aware of Goll grabbing him as he swayed.

'Bran,' said Faelán, 'you do not have the temperament to be a druid.'

Bran hurled his bells at the fire, his face livid. He sprang to his feet, shooting darts of hatred at the other fosterlings.

Ket watched in shock as he stormed away. 'But . . . but . . . what about me?' croaked Ket. 'Faelán forgot about me.'

Nessa's Clan

Next morning, Ket was still anxious and bewildered.

'Faelán left me out,' he railed. 'He praised Nessa, and Lorccán and Nath-í, but he didn't have anything nice to say about me.'

'So?' Goll was peering into the bronze cauldron used for brewing remedies. 'Probably, there were so many good things to say, he didn't know where to begin.'

Ket scowled. 'There isn't anything special to say about me. I'm not best at anything.'

'Don't be so dismal. You're good at listening, and you try hard, and . . . and . . .' Goll dropped some large furry mullein leaves into the pot, and stirred them with a stick. 'And you're good at sharing,' he finished lamely.

Ket picked up a stone and stabbed angrily at the ground. 'None of those things are special. I know I'll be the next one he sends away.'

Goll was concentrating on his potion. He lifted the steaming leaves out of the cauldron, and let them drip for a moment off the end of the stick.

'All right, hold out your toes.'

Ket flinched as the hot poultice was slapped onto his bare feet. 'Now, leave it there all day,' ordered Goll, binding a length of twine around. 'And keep your brogues on too.'

Then he was gone, following the druid between the trees, and Ket watched moodily as the two of them glided off over the plain. When they passed the cairn of the Shadow Ones, Ket fancied he heard murmuring from the grave. He turned with a shudder and crossed the clearing to the Sacred Yew to lour at the ogham rod with its baffling message.

'We need more clues!' he exclaimed in frustration as Nessa strolled over to join him.

But Nessa seemed uninterested in the rod. She eyed Ket, chewing her lip, and tugging one of her braids.

'Ket, I . . . I made up a poem about you.'

He stared at her.

Nessa puffed out her cheeks. 'Well . . . Here it is. It's not very good.

Brave as a spear
He's straight of aim.
He faces fear
And dares shame.
He joins a fight
With all his might . . .'

Her voice trailed away and she cleared her throat. 'That's all, so far.'

Ket tried to answer. He swallowed.

'Hey, what have you found out?' Lorccán came rushing over and looked down eagerly at the birch rod.

Nessa blinked at him. 'We weren't talking about the ogham,' she said.

'Huh.' Lorccán raised his eyebrows disbelievingly and stalked off.

Nessa shrugged and turned back to Ket. 'Master Faelán says I can visit my clan and find out what's happening with Gortigern and Tirech. Do you want to come with me?'

A bitter wind was driving across the plain, and howling around the cairn, but Ket felt warmed inside by a glow of pride and happiness. As the wind gusted them along, he kept glancing at Nessa, wanting to say thank you, but too shy.

Where the rocky ground gave way to bog, the first

ringforts came into sight. The trackway of logs was half submerged in the soft mud, and Nessa caught hold of Ket's hand. Her fingers were icy. He clung tightly, still not speaking. But as they picked their way through the mire, he tried to send her a message with the pressure of his grasp.

Mosses and lichens grew like a woolly fleece of grey and green all around them. They could hear the trilling of skylarks and meadow pipits, and the occasional plaintive *wheep* of a golden plover. Here and there were high tufts of heather and deer grass, the russet leaves of bog cotton, and the golden seed heads of asphodel.

Suddenly, a snipe exploded under their feet, flying up in a blur of wings.

Ket and Nessa jumped in fright.

'I nearly trod on it!' Ket exclaimed.

'We haven't been paying proper attention,' said Nessa. 'We've been forgetting to look and listen the way Faelán told us to.'

Now, with earnest eagerness, they kept stopping to examine things. They ran the long stalks of heather through their fingers, feeling the softness of the tiny pointed leaves.

'And aren't the flowers pretty?' said Ket. Though their vibrant hues had faded, the dead flower heads had dried into delicate, almost transparent bells.

The two friends stopped to peer into a pit, where

peat had been gouged out of the bog for fuel. The scar, with its straight, cut edges, glistened dark brown. From the centre, protruded a jagged, silvery tree stump.

'Pity we don't have an axe,' said Nessa. 'Master Faelán would have praised us for bringing back some of that wood.'

But Ket was glad they couldn't. He gazed uneasily at the frozen, contorted shapes of the roots. Faelán had told them that pine trees no longer grew in Ireland. This one had lain in the bog for thousands of years, and now here it was, exposed. To him, the pit seemed like a grave that had been broken open. Caught on one knotty protuberance was a brass earring and Ket hoped it was an offering to appease the angry Spirits of the Marsh.

'Hey!' yelled a voice.

A strip of crimson cloth came dancing towards them on the breeze. Nessa jumped up to catch it and turned to look. 'That's come from my place,' she cried, waving excitedly to a ringfort where women were tying coloured buntings to the palisades that crested the ramparts.

'Fáilte, fáilte,' called the women.

As the two friends crossed the ditch and entered the yard, dogs leapt and barked in greeting.

'Nessa!' cried her mother, bouncing towards them. Nessa stood stiff and awkward while Egem embraced her. 'My, you grow taller every time I see you! But look at you, you're too thin.' Ket eyed his friend and saw that Egem was right. Nessa's cheeks were hollow, her chin almost as sharp as a knife point. 'You don't get enough to eat at that place,' tutted her mother.

Nessa shrugged. 'It's winter,' she said. 'We'll find more to eat when the warm weather comes. But tell me, what are you hanging up all those coloured rags for?'

'The king, of course. He'll come past here on his way to the chieftain's,' said Egem, stroking Nessa's arm. 'Come inside, both of you.' She began to shepherd them towards the house. 'I'm sure you'd like something to eat.'

'Yes please!' said Ket.

Nessa and Egem bustled into the house, but as Ket reached the doorway, he stopped short, surprised by a feeling of uneasiness. It was a long time since he'd been inside a house. Then the sound of Nessa's happy voice, the warmth of the fire and inviting smells of cooking called out to him, and he hurried through the door.

Egem placed wheaten bread, a jug of honey and a dish of butter in front of them. Ket closed his eyes as he bit into the crust, savouring the salty, creamy taste of the butter.

Nessa nudged him, and broke off a piece of bread to toss on the burning peat – an offering to the Spirit of the Hearth. Ket coloured, embarrassed that he had forgotten.

'Did Tirech get his payment?' asked Nessa, brushing crumbs from her lap. 'Did Gortigern give him the calf?'

'Of course not.' Egem snorted. 'Gortigern refused.'

'But he *can't* refuse. It was the brehon's order!'

Egem shrugged. 'That bully does what he likes, and what can Tirech do?'

'Well he can't just let Gortigern get away with it! I'm going to see Brehon Áengus. *He* can do something!' Nessa shoved her food aside and stood up. 'Where's Uncle Tirech now?'

'With the other men, busy mending the road for the king,' said Egem. 'But . . . here . . .' The plate wavered in her hand as Nessa charged out the door.

'Thank you!' Ket grabbed a slice of bread in each hand.

As he stepped out into the fresh, cold air again, he felt a quiver of relief and looked eagerly around, checking the clouds, the wind, the position of the sun. He could no longer feel comfortable hemmed in by walls and a roof.

The ringfort stood on the crest of a hill. From here, low drystone fences stretched beyond the ramparts, like spokes from the hub of a wheel. They enclosed the pastures where cattle and sheep grazed, the orchard, the vegetable garden and the crop fields, bare now for the winter. On the slopes beyond, there were other ringforts dotted about, and Ket and Nessa could see small figures toiling on the trackway that ran between them. The men were splitting oak logs to lay across a bed of brushwood and stones. The steady *thump-thumps* as they beat the wedges into the logs drifted up to the ringfort.

'There's Uncle Tirech,' cried Nessa, pointing. 'But come on, we're going to see the brehon.'

Brehon Áengus chewed a haunch of mutton as Nessa spoke, then laid down the bare bone, and heaved a contented sigh. His whiskers and round cheeks were shiny with grease.

'Well now,' he pronounced, 'if Gortigern the Intruder has not paid his fine, Tirech must give notice of distraint. I must accompany him as witness.' The lawgiver picked up a brimming mead cup and drank deeply.

'And then, does Uncle take the calf?' asked Nessa.

'Oh no.' Áengus thumped the cup down, and wiped his dripping moustache with the back of his hand. 'Legally, Gortigern will have five days to respond. He may choose to settle the matter at once, or he may give a pledge to signify his willingness to settle the matter in the future.'

A serving girl offered the lawgiver a platter of cheese.

'Ah.' He stabbed at the large round lump with his knife, and looked at the two figures standing expectantly in front of him. 'Not today, not today.' He waved them away. 'You can see I am occupied. Anyway, night is nearly upon us. Tell Tirech to see me in the morning.' He popped a hunk of the cheese in his mouth and lifted the mead cup again.

Out by the trackway, the men had stopped work for the day. They were weary and mud-spattered, but the new-laid surface of split logs stretched before them in a long, gleaming line. Tirech raised his eyebrows when Nessa gave him the message.

'We'll see,' he growled.

They watched him plod off towards his home.

'It's not fair,' Nessa complained. 'I won't be here tomorrow; I won't know what happens.'

Darkness was gathering and the fierce wind whipped their faces, as the two friends headed back to camp. Ket thrust forward, exhilarated by the strength of the spirits he could feel in the air. The wind carried strange scraping and thumping noises down the slope towards them.

'What's going on?' panted Nessa.

At the edge of the camp, they stopped, startled. In the yellow light of the flames, the anruth were piling up stones into something that looked like a small cairn. For a heart-stopping moment, Ket thought Faelán had died, but then he saw the tall, bearded figure by the fire. The druid was holding a bushy branch in his hand and sweeping it through the air, his long hair and cloak streaming out behind him.

'Spirits of the Ai-i-r,' he called, his voice almost carried away by the howling of the gale.

Ket and Nessa watched in bewilderment, pulling their cloaks tight around them. In the gathering darkness, the figures of the anruth still staggered across the clearing, their arms loaded with stones.

Faelán strode forward, weaving the branch through the air, then cast it on the fire. 'Dispel wind! Dispel!'

He stood with his arms upheld, glowering around him. The wind gave a few more fitful gusts, then ebbed away. Faelán squatted by the fire and held out his hands to the warmth. Behind him, the pile of stones was now higher than his head.

'Hey, what's happening? What are you all doing?' Ket tried to grab Goll's sleeve as he stumped past lugging a large boulder.

'Building a house. For the master,' said Goll shortly.

'A *house*? For *Faelán*?' Ket and Nessa stared at each other. 'But . . . but . . .'

'He's getting old. The cold bothers him.'

'But . . . but druids don't . . .'

'Come and help,' grunted Goll, 'instead of standing there stuttering.'

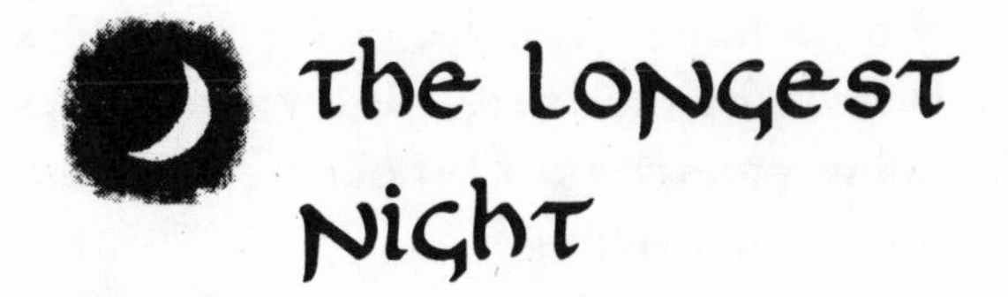

The Longest Night

The morning was so icy, Ket could not feel his fingers. He tucked his hands under his armpits and sat in the darkness listening to the dawn chorus of the birds. He recognised their different voices calling from the trees around him: the *plinking* of a blackbird, the chirrup of a chaffinch, and then, drowning them all, the loud, persistent trill of the wren.

Weak, watery daylight crept over the world at last, and Ket spied the tiny wren perched on a gorse bush. Its feathers were fluffed out for warmth, and it was wagging its tail from side to side as it sang.

Everything around was covered with frost. Sparkling crystals whitened bushes, and crusted bare branches. Ket huffed, and his breath hung in a white vapour in the freezing air.

He glanced at the stone hut, still discomforted by the sight of a building in the middle of camp. Within those walls, how could the druid know what was happening in the world around him?

Ket turned his face to the sun, but there was no warmth in its rays. He looked at the leafless trees. He thought of Nessa's hollow cheeks, of the brambles stripped of berries, of the bare, muddy riverbanks without a shoot of watercress or brooklime. Suddenly, he could be patient no longer.

'Master Faelán,' he called, 'the sun is dying. The trees are dying. When . . . when are you going to do something?'

Around him, the sleeping figures stirred and groaned. Nessa's head popped out of her cover and she blinked at Ket with wide, shocked eyes.

Lorccán sat up, grinning. 'Well, you've really done it now,' he whispered. 'Master Faelán is going to *eat* you!'

There was a rustling inside the hut, and Ket watched the doorway nervously.

When Faelán appeared, there were dried stalks clinging to his clothes, for his floor was padded with rushes. To Ket's relief, he was smiling.

'Ah, you are observant, my Ket. And yes, you are right. Winter has become king. It is time for us to intervene. Today we must sacrifice the wren.'

'Why a wren?' asked Lorccán. 'Why not something bigger, like an eagle? Or what about a stag, with those huge antlers?'

'The wren is the voice of winter, and winter must be vanquished.'

Ket glanced at the creature singing happily on the gorse bush.

'They're such fragile little birds,' he said.

'Yes,' Nessa agreed. 'They don't *look* important.'

'Maybe not, but the wren is king of the birds. Do you not know the tale of the wren and the eagle?' asked Faelán.

The fosterlings shook their heads.

'Then that will be the tale you learn today.'

When Maura brought her master a bowl of breakfast gruel, Faelán faced the fire and intoned, 'Thank you, Spirit of the Hearth, for your heat.' He looked towards the woods. 'And thank you, Spirit of the Forest, for our sustenance.'

Ket peered into his own bowl and grimaced. It was hard to feel grateful for a few sprigs of chickweed floating in boiling water.

The druid took a sip, and steam wreathed his face as he told the tale.

'Fortune favours those who recount a tale faithfully,' he began, as he always did. 'One day, all the birds of the forest gathered to choose their king. The birds agreed that the one who could fly highest would be their sovereign.' Faelán cocked an eyebrow at his listeners. 'Which bird do you think that will be?'

'The eagle!' they all answered together.

Faelán smiled and set down his bowl.

'Well, the eagle strove his utmost. He beat his wings with all his might, and he rose wellnigh to the sun. "See me", he called, "I am the king!" But when all the other birds were looking his way, another tiny head peeked out from the eagle's crest. It was the wren, riding on the eagle's back. Then the wren flapped his wings and raised himself above the eagle. The wren was king!'

'Clever!' said Nessa.

'Tonight, as you know,' said Faelán, 'we hold a mock battle between the wren and the robin. The robin, with its fiery red breast, will take the part of the sun, and the robin will conquer the wren.'

'This year, can I be the robin?' asked Lorccán.

The druid regarded him thoughtfully. 'Why not? And you, Ket, can be the wren. You can show me what you've been learning in your weapon-training with Maura. Now, finish your breakfast quickly. You must carry the message around the tuath.'

In a flurry of excitement, the four fosterlings

wound holly sprigs through their hair. They looked at each other admiringly. The berries glowed in their hair like tiny crimson suns, and the lushness of the evergreen leaves was a promise of the rebirth that would come to the land with the strengthening of the sun.

Art and Bronal plunged among the gorse bushes and when they emerged, Bronal was clutching a brown, feathered shape in his fist. With solemn ritual, the druid laid it on the altar and called for the blessing of the spirits.

'Now, Ket, I entrust this into your keeping,' said Faelán.

The fosterlings hurried off, Ket proudly bearing the sacrificial wren, still warm, in his hands. The pathetic little bundle was a sign to all that today would see the death of winter. Every household they reached sent messengers to other ringforts and, in the brief hours of daylight, the word spread throughout the tuath.

Returning at nightfall, the fosterlings found the anruth stacking a mountainous heap of firewood on the plain. Goll fetched a flame from the druid's fire and thrust it into the heap. For a moment, the little flame burned brightly, then it burrowed its way into the deep, dark mass of branches, and disappeared. Everyone held their breaths.

'Come on, fire, come *on*,' urged Nessa.

They waited in a tense, expectant circle.

'It's no good. It's gone out,' said Nath-í.

But Lorccán let out a shout. 'Look!' he cried, pointing. Then they all saw a tongue of flame licking the side of the pile.

Beyond it, a blaze of yellow crackled up, then another, and another. Lorccán was dancing around in excitement. 'Look . . . look!'

A branch fell in a sputter of sparks, and now at last the whole, huge bonfire roared into life.

The druid joined them. He wore a massive gorget of flattened gold, crescent-shaped and wide as a hand span. Brilliant in the leaping flames, it looked like a sun hanging around his neck.

Dots of light, like fallen stars, pierced the distant darkness, and suddenly, from all around, a galaxy of tiny bobbing flames was flowing towards them. The people of the tuath were gathering. Ket felt excitement and pride blaze inside him, as fierce as the burning bog pine in his hand. As they reached the circle of firelight he could see the children, clinging to their mothers' hands, or riding on their fathers' shoulders, all wide-eyed with wonder, and every one of them carrying a torch or candle to coax back the sun.

When the whole tuath was assembled, Faelán heaved an oak log into the heart of the flames. A shower of bright red embers swirled through the air. The throng fell silent.

'May the log burn
May the wheel turn
May the sun return,'
chanted the druid.

And so the vigil for the longest night of the year began. Hour upon hour the people sang, talked and kept watch. The lights of their torches and candles slowly dwindled, but the fire still burned bright.

'Ket!' Nessa exclaimed, coming to sit beside him. 'I asked Uncle Tirech what happened. And you'll never guess! Gortigern wouldn't let him take a calf – of course – but he paid a pledge instead, and do you know what that bully used for a pledge?'

Ket blinked with tiredness. 'Tell me.'

'His own baby! Can you imagine? Gortigern handed over his two-year-old son!' Nessa's eyes glittered in the firelight.

Ket tried to look interested, but before he could prevent it, his jaws stretched open in a huge yawn. He glanced at Nath-í curled up on the ground asleep, and his own body sagged. Propping his head against Nessa's shoulder, he closed his eyes.

'Just for a moment,' he murmured.

When he opened them again, Nessa was asleep too, and the singing had stopped. There was darkness all around, except for the bonfire. The anruth were busy stoking up the flames, and Ket saw, with a pang, that Lorccán was helping them. Lorccán was the only fosterling who had not fallen asleep.

'Here, Ket, spread the light,' said Maura. 'I was just about to wake you.' She handed him a bundle of peeled rushes soaked in grease. 'Kindle these, and hand them around. And rouse the others. They can help.'

In a few minutes, there was a ripple of light spreading through the crowd, and a stir of anticipation. Ket was alert now, taut and on edge.

'Lorccán and Ket, it is time for your battle,' said Faelán.

Ket watched with envy as Lorccán, the robin, was dressed in a red léine. In one hand he carried a shield gleaming with white paint, and in the other a shiny new sword. When Lorccán pranced into the cleared space by the fire, the crowd roared its approval.

Now it was Ket's turn. He pulled a face as a torn, faded tunic was tugged over his head. The wren was supposed to look feeble and old. He was given a battered shield, the wood split and unpainted, and a rusty, bent sword with a wobbly hilt.

When Ket stepped into the light, and heard the hisses and boos of the audience, he wanted to throw down his arms and run. Instead, he tightened his grip and turned to his opponent.

Lorccán grinned. 'You've got to lose, remember.'

Ket scowled and clattered his sword against his shield, the way the real warriors did. It rattled loudly, then half the shield broke off and dropped to the ground.

The crowd erupted into laughter and Ket felt his cheeks burning.

'Yah!' yelled Lorccán. He flourished his sword and stabbed at Ket.

'Watch it!' Ket skipped to the side, and took the impact on his broken shield.

'You lose!' screamed Lorccán, thrusting again.

Ket just managed to parry with his wobbly sword.

'Hey, this is just pretend!' he cried, but Lorccán laughed, and lunged again.

Their swords clanged and the next instant they were pressed together, Lorccán's shield against Ket's chest.

The crowd was screaming.

'You're dead!' roared Lorccán. He stepped back and raised his sword.

Ket took one look at the fervour in Lorccán's eyes and threw himself on the ground. 'All right, I'm dead!' he screamed, as Lorccán's blade plunged towards him. It shuddered to a halt, the point almost piercing his neck.

Ket lay rigid, staring into Lorccán's triumphant face, and remembered his father, sprawled on the ground at Morgor's feet.

Lorccán's shield reflected the red of the fire, and his sword flashed gold as he hoisted it in victory.

The crowd stamped and cheered.

'Well done, boys,' said Faelán, as Ket rose unsteadily to his feet. He wrapped an arm round each of their shoulders. 'That was very convincing. Now, Nessa ...' He turned to look for her. 'Cast the wren into the fire.'

Nessa stepped forward and in a few minutes the small feathered body was devoured by the flames.

Faelán looked at the dark sky and they all followed his gaze.

'May Winter die
May the Sun be free
Bring life to the land
And leaf to the tree,'

he called.

The anruth and fosterlings repeated his words.

'Bring life to the land
And leaf to the tree.'

Around the fire, others took up the chant. Somewhere, a drum began to beat.

'May Winter die
May the Sun be free
Bring life to the land
And leaf to the tree.'

The words rose louder and faster, pouring towards the sky. Then the darkness split, and a shimmering line of light burst along the horizon. There was a triumphant tremolo from a wooden whistle, and suddenly everyone was clapping their hands, stomping their feet, twirling, singing and dancing.

The druid beamed at Ket.

'Now, every day, you will see the sun grow stronger,' he promised. 'And soon the green of spring will cloak the land.'

Ket gazed on the multitude of rejoicing people, his heart swelling. It was Faelán, his master, who had brought this outpouring of hope and happiness.

'But some day,' vowed Ket, '*I* will be the one to make them dance!'

King's Visit

Ket gazed enviously at the druid's garb: the feathered cloak, the gold fillet binding his hair, and the bronze snake with garnet eyes that coiled up his arm. He gave a disgruntled tweak to his own knee-length tunic, roughly stitched from undyed wool, and wished he had something more suitable to wear for visiting a king. If he'd been an anruth now, he'd have a long grey robe and a circlet of silver around his head. He knelt by the river, scooped some of the freezing water over his head, and tried to comb the tangled mass of his hair with his fingers.

As they set off for Morgor's ringfort, he glanced at the rest of the retinue. Nessa was dressed in a new robe she'd made for herself, dyed yellow with apple bark. As usual, her hair was neatly braided and beaded in gold. Her nails were coloured with berry juice, and earrings of crimson rowan berries hung over her ears. She looked like a princess. Lorccán's shimmering fair hair always hung smooth, and he looked so proud no one noticed what he wore. As for Nath-í . . . Ket grinned and felt better. At least his own garments were less torn and stained than Nath-í's.

They took the route over the plain and through the bog. Crossing the marshy ground, there were squeals and laughter as everyone hopped from plank to plank, trying not to splash in the mud. Nobody was surprised when Nath-í, with a rueful cry, slid knee-deep into the mire.

Only the druid walked with dignity. Ket watched him, intrigued. Even when his feet touched the mud, they left no mark on the moist, yielding surface. He led the way with sure, steady tread, until he stopped abruptly, cocking his head. They all listened. From somewhere to their right came three short cries of a raven.

'Is it an omen?' asked Nessa in a hushed voice.

The druid turned. His colourless eyes were glittering like two raindrops caught in the sunlight.

'Someone in this party will reap great honour from this occasion,' he said.

The fosterlings continued for a short distance in subdued silence, glancing speculatively at each other.

Then they reached the pale patch of new-laid track and burst into renewed chatter, scurrying forward.

Nessa cast a glance at the ringfort of her Uncle Tirech.

'I wonder what's been happening?' she muttered. 'Do you think he's got the calf yet?'

Morgor's fort looked as grand as the dun of a king. They gazed across the fields at ramparts of stone higher and wider than those of any ringfort they'd passed.

'Hey, isn't that Bran?' cried Nessa.

In the middle of a pasture stood a familiar figure minding a troop of fat, contented cows. He didn't answer when they waved and shouted.

They all fell silent with awe as they drew near the imposing ramparts. There were wooden lookouts built into the walls; and archers watched their approach, with bows drawn.

'And there's *more*!' whispered Nath-í as they clattered onto the bridge over the ditch.

Sure enough, when they filed out of the tunnel through the immense stone wall, they saw another ditch, and another rampart.

'Nobody could break in here!' said Lorccán, eyes wide with admiration.

Ket glanced at the druid. He was stroking his beard musingly.

In the yard there was a kiln for drying grain, and a granary so brimful of barley, rye and oats that kernels were overflowing out the door onto the cobblestones. The pigsty was full to bursting, and in the calf-pen the yearlings stood shoulder to shoulder, jostling for space.

The chieftain's hall sprawled in the centre of it all. It was not round, like a normal house, but had long, straight walls, covered with a white coating. Dozens of people were milling around the yard, though it seemed there were even more inside, for the noise coming from the hall sounded loud enough to blow the roof from its rafters.

Nath-í and Ket drew close to Nessa as they stepped over the threshold. There were crowds of people slurping mead or ale and shouting to be heard, their voices slurred and raucous. Lorccán trotted at Faelán's side, smiling and waving as people reeled out of the druid's way.

The air was hazy with smoke, and filled with the fumes of food and drink. A whole boar rotated on a spit on the huge hearthfire in the middle of the room, fat trickling down to hiss and smoke in the flames. Nath-í and Ket stopped walking to stare. Ket was so hollow he felt as if his stomach was clamped against his backbone.

'Ket!' A hand gripped Ket's shoulder, and he turned to find his father looking down at him. Ossian jerked his head at the spit. 'Impressive, hey?' Ossian gave a wry smile. 'Morgor has surpassed himself this year.'

Before Ket could answer, his uncles, Ailbe and Senach, sharing a huge mead cup, came rolling up to bear Ossian away.

As the druid and his followers threaded their way down the hall, a strange figure leapt in front of them, capering on the rush-strewn floor. He was dressed in a ridiculously short léine; heavy gold rings swung on his ears, and he wore a speckled white cloak. He tossed a dagger in the air, then another, and another and began to juggle wildly. Around the hall, the drunken applause was deafening.

Beyond the juggler, through the smoke, Ket could see the king on a dais at the end of the hall, with Morgor at his left hand. King Breasal had white-blond hair and lush, drooping whiskers. He wore a heavy crown and his arms were loaded from elbow to wrist with gold and silver bracelets. His ankle-length robe was purple satin embroidered with silver. His long mantle had been woven from threads of many colours and was fastened with a brooch of crystal and bronze. A huge shield hung on the wall behind him.

'Welcome, Druid of the Forest,' called Morgor, as they approached.

'Ah, the druid is come. Do you bring poems or prophecies this day?' asked the king.

'Should Your Majesty desire a prophecy,' Faelán replied, 'I have my tools of divination.' He tapped the pouch at his belt. 'And here . . .' he gestured to the fosterlings 'are four admirers to sing your praises.'

The king inclined his head. 'And I have a gift for you, O Druid. Morgor tells me you have no footwear, so I ordered my silversmith to make you these . . .'

He lifted one finger and a man stepped forward. In his hands was a pair of sandals with thick soles of silver and glittering silver ornaments dangling from the laces.

Ket slid his eyes sideways to catch the druid's expression. To his surprise, Faelán beamed with pleasure and allowed a servant to tie the sandals to his feet. He was now taller than anyone else in the room.

The chieftain looked up at him with pride on his face. 'Will you honour this assembly with a prophecy?' he asked.

'To what question do you seek an answer?'

Morgor gestured around the room. 'My household,' he said. 'What does the future hold for my household?'

The druid held out his pouch.

'Make a selection and I will divine the answer.'

'A prophecy, a prophecy!' Knives thumped on tables. Everyone craned forward.

Morgor plunged his hand in the pouch and drew out a rod.

ᚈ

'That's ogham!' hissed Nath-í.

'But it's one we already know,' Lorccán complained.

The druid took the feda in his hand and studied it.

'*Tinne,*' he murmured.

There was a breathless hush.

Then Faelán held up the rod for all to see. 'This is the symbol for battle and bloodshed!' he declared.

There were exclamations around the room.

Morgor rubbed his hands.

'Ha, we have nothing to fear. The Ardal clan will conquer all!'

Faelán smiled enigmatically. 'And now,' he announced, 'the poems in honour of King Breasal.'

The room fell silent apart from a few befuddled cheers.

The fosterlings glanced at each other, then Lorccán stepped forward and stretched his arms wide.

'No measly weasel
Is King Breasal!'
he announced, and made a flourishing bow.

Ket and Nessa avoided each others' eyes, trying not to laugh for, unfortunately, the king did look rather like a weasel.

Nessa pinched his arm. 'Come on, Ket,' she whispered.

They stepped forward together. Ket cleared his throat.

'Bountiful as an oak laden with acorns
Tough as an alder shield in battle
Strong as elm in the hull of a ship
Is King Breasal.'
they recited in unison.

Ket squirmed with embarrassment, but the king looked satisfied, and in the sea of faces Ket caught a glimpse of his father smiling proudly.

Now it was Nath-í's turn. Faelán's eyes lit up with expectation, and he reached for his harp. Surprised, the others turned to look. Nath-í was kneeling in his mud-caked trews, head thrown back, and the plum sign on his cheek clearly visible. As music rippled from the harp, he broke into song.

'King Breasal glows
Like a star in the night
I bow my knee
To his shining light

King Breasal is famed
Throughout the land
For his fearless heart
And his generous hand
When the kings all gather
On Uisnech hill
The others will bow
To Breasal's will.'

There was a moment of silence, then everyone in the room began to whistle and clap. Ket sucked in his breath as King Breasal rose to his feet and slid a wide gold bracelet from his arm. He leaned across the table and held it out to Nath-í.

'Well done, young bard,' he said. He glanced at the druid. 'Faelán, you have a fine pupil there. You must value him very highly.'

Ket felt the familiar sinking feeling in the pit of his stomach.

More subjects arrived to pay their respects and taxes to the king, and the fosterlings were jostled aside.

'I'm going to get the news from my clan,' said Nessa, and she slipped into the boisterous throng.

For a few bewildering moments, Ket seemed to be in everyone's way. People elbowed past him, trod drunkenly on his feet, thumped him with their swinging sacks, and sent gusts of ale-breath in his face. Then the trumpeter sounded his horn and the rechtaire began directing people to the tables along the walls. He pointed Ket to the lowliest end, near the door. Nessa and Lorccán were there already, behind a table of bare boards, with platters of rough-hewn yew. Along the opposite wall, the tables had linen cloths and dishes of gold and silver. There sat the queen with her ladies, and several men from the clans. Ket saw his father and uncles, and other people he knew – Ragallach, who could have been his foster father, and Brehon Áengus, and Tirech and Gortigern from the clan of Ardal.

'Where's Nath-í?' asked Ket, sliding onto the bench beside Nessa.

Silently, Nessa pointed to the end of the room.

Ket leaned forward to see the dais. A sword-length to the left of the king sat his host, Morgor. And a sword-length to the right, seated with Faelán in the place of honour, was Nath-í!

There was a bitter taste in Ket's mouth as he dragged his eyes away and turned back to Nessa.

'I spoke to Uncle Tirech,' Nessa whispered. 'And he's still stuck with that baby. He's furious. The poor little thing just cries all the time, and piddles all over the house.'

'But why has he still got the baby?' Ket asked. 'It's been *days*. Why doesn't Tirech go back and demand the payment?'

'From Gortigern?' asked Nessa, her voice rising

in astonishment. 'You don't demand anything from Gortigern. Look at him!'

Ket looked at Nessa's kinsmen seated at the opposite table. Gortigern took up the space of two normal men, and his hands, raising the mead cup, were as big as the swollen udders of a cow.

'He's the best fighter in our clan,' Nessa continued. 'And that lazy brehon's no use. I've promised to ask Master Faelán what to do.'

The trumpet sounded again and Ket looked expectantly at King Breasal. But it was Faelán the Druid of the Forest who rose to his feet. Ket felt a thrill of pride. It was true. A druid took precedence even over a king.

'Welcome to each and every one of you,' said Faelán. 'I take this opportunity to thank Morgor for hosting this feast. I thank the Spirits of the Hearth and the generous Earth for their bounty. I thank the animals that gave their lives that we might eat. I now call on the rannaire to perform his duties.'

The boy attending the spit skipped out of the way, and the rannaire stepped forward, brandishing his carving knife. Flames leapt up with a loud hiss as he sliced into the juicy carcass. He slapped the first portions onto a platter, and the attendant staggered with them to the dais. The king and the druid were served, and then an eager silence fell as Breasal scanned the hall.

'Who is worthy of the hero's joint?' demanded the king.

A babble of excited chatter broke out, some voices rising loud and angry, then Gortigern mac Ardal, with a flourish of his cloak, sprang atop the table brandishing his dagger. Dishes flew from under his feet, and clanged to the floor.

'I'm the champion!' he roared.

'Go, Gortigern!' squealed someone.

But another burly figure rose in his seat. 'I challenge you, Gortigern!' he bellowed. He grasped the side of the table, and with a mighty heave sent it clattering on its side.

Gortigern's dagger flew from his grasp as he thudded to the ground. He sprang up, fists raised, as the other fellow bounded over the fallen table and charged him, head lowered like a bull.

'Kill him, Cellach!' cried a few fervent voices.

'Go, Gortigern!' retorted the others.

With a juddering crash the two challengers toppled to the ground, rolling and writhing. Gortigern's sleeve was ripped from his shoulder and his bare arm bulged as he pummelled his opponent. Everyone was on their feet now, cheering their heroes.

Gortigern's flailing hand fell on his dagger and he raised it in the air. The cries in the room rose to hysterical fervour.

'Go! Go! Go!'

The blade flashed and stabbed and a cursing Cellach rolled away, spouting blood.

'Gortigern, Gortigern, Gortigern!' The screams rose to a crescendo as the fighter staggered to his feet brandishing his bloodied dagger. Cellach wormed his way to the side of the room, scattering a trail of red among the rushes.

Ket clambered down from his table, his voice hoarse with screaming. Lorccán was ecstatic.

'Did you see those muscles?' he demanded.

'I told you he was strong!' cried Nessa, her eyes shining.

Ket stared at her, dumbfounded.

'I thought you didn't like Gortigern,' he said.

Nessa tilted her chin. 'He's my kinsman!' she said.

'But . . . he didn't fight fairly,' protested Ket.

'The main thing was, he won!' crowed Lorccán.

'And Faelán's prophecy came true already,' said Nessa. 'Battle and bloodshed!'

Everyone was relaxed and laughing now. The attendant carried a thigh portion of boar to the preening Gortigern, and another to the queen, then moved down the room with the rest of the meat. Other serving lads hurried around, bringing more platters filled with tasty delights: small round mulach cheeses, intestines stuffed with minced flesh, blood and herbs, boiled goose with apple sauce, and cranberry tarts.

'Bet I eat the most!' said Lorccán, piling his plate with food.

The queen rose from her seat and drifted around the room. Ket glanced up from sucking on a neck bone, to find her looking down at them.

'You children did very well with your poetry. Keep up your efforts.' Three slender silver bangles were slid from her wrist and dropped on the table in front of them. As Ket picked his up, he couldn't help thinking of the heavy band of gold now adorning Nath-í's arm.

A wooden mead cup, bigger than Ket's head, was passed down the table towards them.

'Mm,' said Lorccán, smacking his lips, 'that's a man's drink.'

Nessa took a sip and made a face. 'Yuck, you can have it.'

Ket took a big gulp and almost choked. Secretly he agreed with Nessa, but he took another swallow and wiped his mouth with the back of his hand the way the men did. He wondered how honey and apples could be made to taste so disgusting.

A sulky-looking boy was working his way down the table, serving sauce from a bronze jug.

'Hey, look at that, it's Bran!' grinned Lorccán.

'Oh no, he's going to *hate* being our serving boy,' said Nessa.

'How are you?' she asked brightly, as he reached

their end of the table.

There was a shock of envy in Bran's face as he spied her silver bangle. Instantly, Nessa pulled it off and held it out to him.

'Here, I don't want this, you have it,' she said.

Ket saw Bran flinch, and felt the other boy's pain. Their eyes locked and Ket remembered Bran's unexpected sympathy the day of the brehon's visit, the day Nath-í had made Ket look a fool.

'But Bran would hate it if I showed *him* pity,' thought Ket.

'Hey, Bran!' he exclaimed. 'You're so lucky; this place is just like a king's palace. And look at all the food! Do you get to eat like this all the time?' He babbled on, watching Bran anxiously. 'Do you sleep in here at night? And . . . Nessa, Lorccán, did you see his clothes? Look at all that gold embroidery!'

At last, to Ket's relief, Bran lifted his chin and threw a disparaging glance at Nessa's bangle.

'Silver trinket,' said Bran in his old scornful way. 'Here, you'd better eat as much as you can while you've got the chance!'

With gusto, he emptied the contents of his jug over their plates, drowning their food with sauce, and stalked off.

First Snowdrop

'Hey, look what I found!' Lorccán charged into camp brandishing a stalk with a white flower bobbing at the end. 'A snowdrop!' he yelled. 'Look! I found the first snowdrop!'

'Aha.' A smiling Faelán strode forward to meet him. 'You shouldn't have picked it, but well done.' He ruffled Lorccán's hair. 'You are a fine observer.'

Ket clenched his fists. Days ago he had seen tiny green tips of new shoots poking through the soil. He'd been watching and waiting for the buds to open. It wasn't fair that Lorccán had spied the first flower.

Lorccán swanned around the camp, showing his

find to everyone. 'Hey, Nath-í, make up a poem about me!'

Obediently, Nath-í sat down and began to mutter behind his fringe.

Ket wandered across to the Sacred Yew and scowled down at the ogham rod. The message was almost as mysterious now as when Faelán had first inscribed those black marks in the birchwood.

'Got you beaten, hasn't it?' said Lorccán behind him. 'I've found lots of clues. I'm going to be the first one to read it.'

A large black rook glided past with slow, leisurely wingbeats. There was a twig clamped in its beak.

'The rooks are nesting!' cried Nessa. 'That's another sign that spring is coming.' She looked round eagerly for the druid. 'It'll be the Festival of Imbolc soon, won't it?'

The druid nodded. 'At the next full moon.'

Ket saw Nessa glance meaningly at Maura, and the older girl opened her mouth.

'Master, why don't we have Nessa as the Spirit of Spring this year?' asked Maura.

Ket held his breath. Imbolc was after the next new moon.

'Why not?' said Faelán.

Ket looked at his best friend, struggling desperately to conjure up a feeling of joy instead of the envy and dismay that was creeping over him.

Then Nath-í struck another blow.

'I've done it, Lorccán, I've made up a poem about you,' he called eagerly. 'Listen. "The Finding of the First Snowdrop!"'

As he recited it, with Lorccán preening and everyone else listening admiringly, Ket found himself sinking into a sea of gloom.

That night, when they gathered for storytelling, he could barely mumble his way through his part.

'Ket, why didn't you learn your words?' Nessa scolded him afterwards. 'What's the matter with you?'

'There's no point any more,' he growled.

'What do you mean?'

'You know why.'

'Ket, don't be silly. Master Faelán won't send *you* away.'

'No? Then who's he going to choose? Nath-í the brilliant poet? Or Lorccán, his golden-haired pet?'

Nessa stared at him, her face whitening. She couldn't answer.

Next day, Ket's secret clump of snowdrops burst into bloom. 'You're too late,' he said with a lump in his throat. He felt like crushing them flat, but the glowing white flower bells and the fresh green stalks were too beautiful.

He fingered the silver bangle at his wrist, thinking of Bran. 'He's been sent away,' he whispered. 'And so has Riona. And now . . .' He looked at the bangle, twisting it round and round, his eyes burning. 'In a few days, I'll be next.'

On the eve of the new moon, Ket sat alone in the forest with his head buried in his arms. He tried to plan what he would do when he was sent away.

'I suppose I'll go to Ragallach's,' he thought, miserably. He pictured the florid man he'd seen at the king's banquet, his bulbous nose and thick, moist lips. 'I guess he'll send me off on fighting raids. All I can do is use a slingshot or a sword. I don't know how to care for crops or animals. But I don't want to kill herdboys and steal cows. I want to be a druid!'

Into his head flashed an image of the stately, powerful Faelán gently transferring a woodlouse to Riona's hand as he imparted his words of wisdom. Ket saw again the circle of fosterlings pressed forward, all with the same hungry eagerness to learn. Pain filled his chest, and tightened his throat. This time tomorrow he'd be at Ragallach's, where there'd be nobody to share his longings and dreams like that.

Now he would never learn the secrets of all the ogham, or how to read the signs in the stars and clouds. And never again would he have the chance to earn the warm approval of the druid's smile.

Faint in the distance, he heard the call of Faelán's bells. It was time.

Sadly, he rose to his feet.

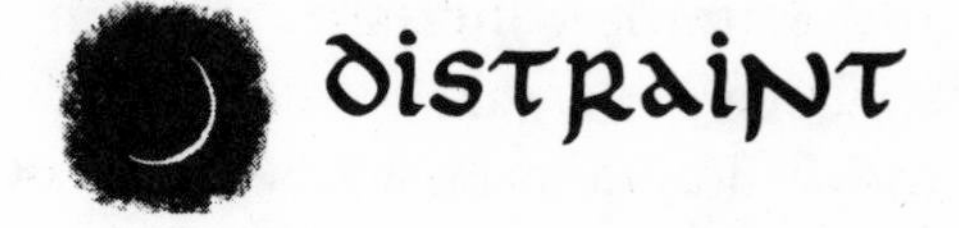

Distraint

Ket halted at the edge of the trees, his heart lurching at the sight of all the people who'd become his family gathered at the fireside. There was tall Goll peering anxiously around for him. There was the chunky figure of Maura beckoning him to hurry. There was Master Faelán, Druid of the Forest, waiting patiently, the feathers in his cloak rippling and changing colour. Even Lorccán, yelling at him to hurry up, was suddenly dear to him. And Art and Bronal and Nath-í. And Nessa . . .

He walked towards them, his branch of bells clutched tight. Nessa handed him a stick of rowan, and as he tossed it into the fire and watched the flames leap up, 'This is the last time,' he thought. 'This is the last time.'

'Spirit of the Moon
Arise from darkness.
Spirit of the Moon
Return and guide us.'

The words rose around him, but Ket's eyes were too blurred with tears to see the new moon in the sky.

When they sat by the fire, Ket was shivering. Nessa, without speaking, wrapped her cloak around both of them. He felt the warmth of her arm across his shoulders as Faelán began to speak.

'Tonight,' said the druid, 'I must sing the praise of one whose talent was hidden for most of his sojourn with us. Nath-í, behind his shy façade, has the spirit of a true poet. Let this be a lesson to all of you to seek below the surface for concealed treasure. I foretell that Nath-í will compose epics that will live throughout the generations, keeping alive forever the memories of our heroes and their achievements. And Nath-í himself will be remembered as the man with the tongue of gold.'

Nath-í's head was bowed, his face concealed by his lank black hair. Lorccán had a confused, wary look on his face.

'Nath-í, I am sure that your skill with words would make you a powerful druid,' said Faelán. 'Nevertheless . . .'

Everyone was completely still, completely silent. A log toppled into the fire with a loud crackle, and Ket jumped.

'Nevertheless,' repeated Faelán, 'that is not to be. Nath-í, King Breasal has requested that you join his entourage to compose more poems in his praise. That is an honourable calling, and one that is eminently suited to your talents. So, tonight you will be the one to leave us, not in disgrace, but to accept the position of the king's bard.'

Nath-í raised his head, looking startled and wary, like a fawn.

'But . . . what about my blemish,' he stammered, touching his cheek. 'Doesn't the king mind?'

'Blemish?!' cried Faelán. 'By oak, ash and thorn, Nath-í, that is no blemish. It is a sign to distinguish you. As your fame grows and spreads, tales will be told of you, and wherever you go, people will recognise you by the sign on your face. "There goes Nath-í of the golden tongue!" they will declare.'

Nath-í's face glowed so fiercely with pride it was as if a fire had been lit behind his eyes.

'And *now,*' said Nessa next morning, 'you can stop sulking, Ket, and come help sort out that problem for my Uncle Tirech.'

Ket laughed. He felt like singing and dancing and flinging things into the air. He felt that if he jumped off the top of a cliff he would float through the air with happiness.

As they headed for Nessa's ringfort, there was a flurry of snow. Ket tilted up his face and caught the snowflakes on his tongue. His feet kept wanting to run and hop. He raced to the top of the cairn without a thought for the dead beneath, let out a wild whoop of joy, then hurtled down again, skittering and sliding, sending stones – and skulls – cascading.

'You're mad,' chuckled Nessa.

They could hear Gortigern's baby wailing as they approached the ringfort. The buntings on the ramparts no longer billowed in colourful celebration but hung limp and sodden. The yard was deserted except for the animals huddled in their pens. A lone dog tied to a post yapped half-heartedly but nobody paid attention. Everyone was indoors, sheltering from the weather.

Nessa and Ket stooped to enter the house. There were two men seated by the firepit playing a board game while children swarmed over them, clambering on the benches and bumping the low wooden table. Nessa's mother had her back to them, working at her loom. Tirech sat by the door, whittling a rowan branch for a new axe-handle while a woman paced beside him trying to soothe the crying baby.

Tirech raised his eyes. 'Nessa!' he rumbled. 'What do you want now?'

'Nessa?' cried Egem, spinning round.

Ket watched hopefully as Nessa's mother bustled towards the hearth and prodded at something in the cooking pot.

Nessa placed her hands on her hips.

'Uncle Tirech, I asked Master Faelán what to do next,' she said.

'Haven't you meddled enough, landing your aunt Dornolla with that brat?' He jerked his chin at the snivelling toddler in his wife's arms.

Ket saw Nessa's cheeks flush.

'You have to keep going,' she said, 'if you want to get your compensation.'

'You tell him, Nessa,' one of the men by the fireside suddenly joined in.

'Yes, Tirech, you got him this far,' called the other. 'What happened to all your big talk about stopping his bullying?'

'Ach, he'll not be bothered with all that, now he's a champion,' growled Tirech. 'He's talking about making himself chieftain next.'

'Huh.' Nessa tossed back her head, and set all her braids jingling. 'He paid you a pledge,' she said. 'What are you going to do with that infant? Sell him as a slave?'

They all looked at the pathetic, whimpering child.

'Of course not,' muttered Tirech. Then he startled everyone by throwing down the axe-handle and stamping to his feet. 'I'll get my calf,' he roared, brandishing his knife. 'You're right. He owes me a debt. And he'll pay me today! Come on. Someone go pry that brehon from his feedbag.'

Table and benches crashed to the ground as the other men jumped to their feet.

'Get him, Tirech,' they bellowed.

'Give him back his brat!' shouted Dornolla.

Egem cheered and waved her serving spoon, sending a spray of hot brothcán sailing through the air.

Afire with indignation, they all streamed onto Gortigern's land, the reluctant brehon in their midst. At the sight of them, a terrified herdboy tried to shout a warning and make a dash for the ringfort, but Nessa caught him by his léine and muffled his cries. The crowd surged through the gate. Gortigern and his brothers burst out of their house, eyes popping with astonishment.

'Dadda!'

There was a shriek from the child in Dornolla's arms and he wriggled to the ground.

Gortigern ignored the little boy toddling towards him. 'What do you want?' he snarled.

Tirech took a deep breath. 'In the presence of the brehon, and these witnesses, I have come to claim my debt!' He took a step towards the calf-pen.

'Don't you dare touch my cows,' roared Gortigern.

Tirech hesitated, and looked back at the brehon.

Suddenly, Nessa's voice rang out.

'Uncle Tirech,' she called, 'Gortigern means he wants to choose the calf himself. Of course he will pay his debt, for he knows that if he fails, he will lose all honour and respect in the eyes of the clan.'

Gortigern stared back at Nessa, and then at the circle of watching faces. Ket held his breath. Slowly, the champion straightened his shoulders, turned on his heel, and stalked towards the pen. He paused a moment, then threw a rope round the neck of a calf. It was a sturdy beast, its reddish coat grown thick and hairy for winter. Gortigern thrust the halter into Tirech's hand.

'That's my best yearling,' he growled. 'Now be off, the lot of you!'

In triumphal procession, Nessa and Tirech led the way from the ringfort.

Festival of Imbolc

'I'm sick of practising slingshot,' Lorccán complained, as Nessa's stone neatly smote the target again. 'Can't we train like the fians? I bet they do more exciting things than aiming stones at apples.'

'They certainly do,' said Maura. 'If you want to train like a fian, I can bury you in the ground up to your waist and give you nothing but a hazel stick and shield to protect yourself. Then we'll all hurl spears at you.'

'Do they really do that?' asked Ket.

Maura nodded.

'I bet I could do it,' said Lorccán.

'What else do they do?' asked Nessa eagerly.

'Race round a tree and try to hit each other with thorn switches,' said Maura.

'Hey, let's try that!' Lorccán sprang to his feet. 'We can use gorse branches. They've got lots of thorns.'

'All right.' Maura agreed. 'But not gorse. We'll start without thorns. Willow whips will be vicious enough. We'll find some by the river.'

They hunted eagerly for young, bendy shoots, but just as Ket raised his knife to cut one down, Maura let out a cry.

'Wait!' She glanced, frowning, at the sky.

'It's all right,' called Ket, 'it's the light half of the month.'

'Yes, of course.'

Ket smiled, proud that he knew what Maura was thinking. Faelán had warned them never to cut willow on a waning moon, for it brought ill fortune. He ran the shoot through his fingers. It was smooth and pliable.

'Yah!' screamed Lorccán, flicking his whip through the air and slapping it on the ground. 'Watch out, everyone!'

'We'll do this in pairs,' said Maura. 'Lorccán, you and Nessa chase each other, and I'll try to catch Ket.'

'Race you to the Sacred Yew,' yelled Lorccán.

'You'll never catch me,' taunted Nessa.

'I'll *slaughter* you!'

'Ket, you and I can use the hollow oak,' said Maura.

Ket eyed the short, dumpy figure bouncing up and down on the other side of the tree.

'Ready?' she called. 'One, two, three . . . coming!'

Maura began to jog towards him and before he had taken two strides, the tip of her whip slashed the ground beside him.

'Yowp!' he yelled. Knees pumping, he spurted forward. When he glanced over his shoulder, Maura was laughing and brandishing the whip again.

'Hurry!' she warned.

'Hurry yourself!' he called back, and raised his whip.

Round and round the tree they raced, shouting and jeering and cracking their whips. At last they both collapsed, laughing, against the tree trunk, their breaths puffing in and out like the bellows of a smith in a forge.

'That . . . was fun,' gasped Ket.

'Oooh,' groaned Maura, holding her side. 'I've got a stitch.'

'Where are the others?'

Ket looked round. They were still chasing each other. Lorccán had a ferocious, intent expression on his face, and kept cracking his whip, but Nessa was keeping well out of his reach.

'All right, you two,' called Maura. 'Enough!'

'If I wasn't going to be a druid, I'd be a champion fian,' said Lorccán, whirling his whip around his head.

'Who *are* the fians?' inquired Nessa, when Ket and Maura panted up to join them. 'Where do they come from?'

Maura waved her arms. 'Everywhere. Some are just discontented boys who have run away from foster families. Others might be outcasts from their clans.'

'How could that happen? Who would be cast out from their own clan?'

Maura shrugged. 'Maybe someone who did something wrong and refused to pay the fine.'

'Like Gortigern!' said Ket.

'Only he did pay up in the end,' Nessa reminded him.

'No clan would dare cast Gortigern out,' said Lorccán with feeling. 'Can you imagine? He'd probably come back and murder them all!'

That night, when they gathered by the fire, Nessa was fizzing with excitement. 'Look!' She gripped Ket's arm as the glowing orb of a full moon appeared in the east.

Faelán smiled down at her.

'Yes, Nessa, it is time for the Festival of Imbolc. Tonight you must sleep in the forest, beside the

Sacred Spring. Maura shall accompany you, and in the morning she will prepare you to perform your part in the ceremony.'

With the two girls gone, the camp felt strange and empty. Ket watched with envy as the druid drew the anruth aside to make preparations that were too secret for the fosterlings to witness. Lorccán wandered off, and scuffed at the fallen leaves by the edge of the forest. Suddenly, he gave an exclamation, and bent down. Ket saw with dismay that he had found the flat stone inscribed with the Cormac name that Ket had cast away. Ket watched apprehensively as the other boy hurried across to the ogham rod to compare the marks. Would Lorccán guess the word that was carved on the stone?

When it came time to sleep, Ket tossed aside his bedding and laid himself straight on the ground with no cover or cushion to separate him from earth or sky. His body grew so cold he could not even feel his face, but he tried to imagine he was a rock, hard and strong.

He slept fitfully, aware all through the night of the empty space beside him. He watched the moon gradually make her way across the sky and wondered how Nessa was faring. The dew began to fall, and he burrowed his fingers into the damp, sweet-smelling soil, pretending he was a young plant thrusting out roots.

He was up before sunrise, piling wood on the fire, and constantly glancing towards the trees, though he knew it was much too early for Nessa to return. Art and Bronal were surprised to find the fire burning merrily when they groaned out of their warm coverings.

At dawn, Faelán emerged from his hut. He settled his best feather cloak about his shoulders, and shod his feet with the silver sandals.

By daylight everyone was awake. They called out excited greetings as visitors began to arrive laden with new-baked loaves, dripping honeycombs, flitches of bacon, pats of fresh, glistening butter, and pails brimming with frothy sheep's milk, the first of the spring.

'Look who's here!' cried Ket.

Riona was peeking from behind a huge wheel of flat bread she held clutched to her chest.

'I made it myself,' she said proudly, as Ket ran to take it from her arms.

'This is going to be the best feast ever!' said Lorccán. 'And I'm ravenous!'

But no one was allowed to swallow a morsel before the Spirit of Spring arrived. They milled restlessly about the camp, making disjointed conversation, and Lorccán took out his impatience by punching Ket on the shoulder whenever he passed.

At last Faelán picked up his harp, and as the first

notes rippled through the air, Nessa appeared between the trees. An awed silence fell on the crowd as she advanced. Her robe was the colour of the soft spring sunshine, and starry golden celandines wreathed her head. Rowan twigs, bursting into bud, were massed in her arms. Walking by her side, Maura waved a branch of hazel on which long yellow catkins bobbed and swayed. They came to a halt beyond the ring of the fire, and Faelán ceased his strumming.

'Bend your knees and bid welcome to the Spirit of Spring!' the druid's voice rang out.

Ket fell to his knees along with all the others and joined the fervent chant.

'O come, Spirit of Spring, you are a hundred times welcome!'

Nessa raised her arms in blessing and the farmers held up spades, hoes and handfuls of seeds. Evergreen leaves of ivy and holly were twined around the handles of their tools.

'May the sowing of your seed bring a fruitful harvest,' said Nessa in a clear, confident voice.

She took her place on a cushion of heather, and a bower of hazel was arranged around her.

Ket shyly kept his distance. This grand maiden didn't seem to be the Nessa he knew.

'And now . . .' urged Faelán with a cry, 'set your spades and hoes to work. Dig the soil . . .'

His words were drowned by the ring of mattocks,

and the scrape of spades. In a few minutes a pit had opened in the earth and everyone crowded to the edge to cast in their offerings. Earrings were torn from ears, pins from cloaks, rings from fingers, and tools hacked in half. Carried away by the fervour around him, Ket tossed in his silver armband from the queen. He watched it spin through the air and drop beside a bronze brooch cast in the shape of a stag. It glittered for one last time before it was buried forever in the belly of the earth.

'Mother Earth,' cried Faelán, raising one of the brimming buckets of sheep's milk, 'we thank you for your returning fruitfulness.' He poured a libation of milk over the churned-up ground. 'We offer you sacrifice and in return we beg your favour for our planting and our harvesting.'

The bucket was passed around, and Ket thought he had never tasted anything so sweet. When Riona lowered the bucket, she had a white moustache of froth on her top lip.

At last, it was time for the feasting. Everyone fell on the spread with boisterous enthusiasm. Ket wolfed down the streaky, smoked bacon, the bread oozing with butter and honey, the barm-brack cakes, and the elderberry wine. He didn't pause till his belly was too full to squeeze in another bite. He looked around, wiping his fingers on his léine, and saw someone speaking to the druid. It was Gortigern the

Champion, from the clan of Ardal. Before moving away, Gortigern eased a twisted gold torque from his neck and handed it to Faelán.

As people staggered to their feet to take their leave, Nessa sat like a queen distributing sprigs of rowan. These charms, blessed by the Spirit of Spring, would hang in every barn to protect the new lambs and calves as they were born.

It was not till the crowds were gone, Riona waving till she was out of sight, that Nessa left her bower to join her friends. As she tore the crown of celandines from her head and plonked down beside them, she was just their Nessa again.

The druid eyed them all, lounging contentedly around the fire.

'Imbolc is a time for visions,' he proclaimed. 'And last night I had a prophetic dream. I saw the chieftain walking through his fields. The harvest was so bountiful there were two ears of grain to every stalk, and the branches of the trees were so laden with fruit they bowed to the ground.'

There was a stir of excitement among his listeners.

'And that is not all,' continued the druid, 'in my dream, the chieftain was not Morgor, grandson of Niall, but Gortigern mac Ardal!'

Ket jolted upright and Nessa let out a squeak of surprise.

'But . . . but it was you who helped Morgor win the lordship,' Ket protested.

'Do you question my vision?!' thundered Faelán. Everyone reeled back at the unexpected snarl of anger. '*I* am the kingmaker!' He sucked in his breath, and smoothed his ruffled feathers like a bird. When he spoke again, his voice was hoarse and low. 'Gortigern is the most deserving,' he growled. 'He is a champion, young, handsome . . . and wealthy. And so, we shall assist Gortigern to wrest the lordship from Morgor.'

He strode away, his sandals going *clink-thud, clink-thud* into their stunned silence.

Ket's mind was a whirl of confusion.

Lorccán snatched up a stick and bounded to his feet.

'We're going to be in a fight!' he cried. He began to skip around, stabbing the air.

'A druid doesn't fight with swords,' Maura rebuked him. 'Faelán will use his magic.'

'One of those word spells?' inquired Nessa, glancing at Ket, 'where he stands on one foot and closes one eye, and points his finger?'

'Don't be silly,' scoffed Lorccán. 'Morgor knows about those. He's built big stone walls to hide behind. We'll have to fight our way in.'

'Not us,' said Goll. 'A druid must live to tell the tale of the battle. He can't risk going into danger.

'But we're not druids yet,' objected Lorccán, 'we're just . . .'

Goll shook his head. 'None of his retinue will join in the fight. That'll be up to Gortigern and the other men in Nessa's clan. We'll just be doing healing potions. And maybe we'll make brain balls.'

'Brain balls? What are they?'

Goll grinned. 'When they kill someone, we mix the brains with sea sand and let it harden into balls. With one of those in a slingshot, they can smash down anything.'

'Yah!' yelled Lorccán, whirling an imaginary slingshot.

Battle Preparation

'Nessa . . .' Ket spoke hesitantly. 'Do you think Gortigern is worthy of being a chieftain?'

'Of course. The druid had a dream.'

'That's what he told us. Only . . .'

Nessa stared at him. 'You sound like Bran! Are you saying he made it up?'

Ket chewed his lip. 'No, of course not.' He pushed away the memory of that new torque of solid gold coiling around the druid's neck.

'Druids don't make things up,' said Nessa firmly.

Ket forgot his doubts in the fever of battle

preparation. The people of the tuath were always raiding each others' cattle or skirmishing over land, but it was only in struggles for power that the druid became involved. Ket had never taken part in a real fight, never even seen a battle, except that once, standing on the ramparts, witnessing his father's humiliation.

'And now Morgor is going to get a taste of his own treatment!' he thought exultantly.

To his pride and excitement, Faelán taught them the rituals for gathering the different healing plants. He instructed them which plants could only be picked after a day of fasting, or gathered with the left hand. He told them when they had to rise before the dawn, and pick while the dew still hung from the leaves. Jubilantly, they brought him the elm branches to make into healing wands, the marsh plants, rowan berries, holly leaves, and willow bark for poultices and potions. They climbed hills to find scarce trees or berries, waded through treacherous bog, and picked till their nails were torn and their fingers bruised.

All around them, the forest rang to the clangour of men chopping wood for shields and weapons. Gleefully, Ket pictured them pouring over Morgor's ramparts, hewing their way through his army, and reducing Morgor to a cowering wreck.

Day after day, the men of the Ardal clan came

stamping into camp, huge and noisy, to thrust long ash branches into the flames and harden them for their spear shafts. They brought their swords and daggers too, for Faelán's blessing, till the whole camp was a dazzling array of shining blades, bronzed sheaths and gleaming golden hilts.

'Hey, look at this one.' Lorccán dropped a bundle of willow bark to reach for the silvery sword, engraved with twirling leaves and flowers, that was propped against the Sacred Yew.

'Lorccán, don't,' protested Nessa.

Lorccán, ignoring her, lifted it and flexed it in his hands.

'Huh!' he said in disgust. 'Look how soft it is.'

To Ket's dismay, he bent the blade, then dumped it down where he had found it. Anxiously, Ket pressed it back into shape.

'Nessa, come and give me a hand,' called Maura.

Gortigern's men were standing in a row, slingshots at the ready, and Maura was about to teach them some of her tricks. Nessa, tall and lithe, took her place and swung her slingshot. Ket caught his breath. Nessa was like a red-gold flower swaying and twirling in the wind.

'Hey, Ket, if you've got time to stand around gawking, you've got time to help me,' called Art. He staggered past, his arms loaded with wood. 'Come on, we need more rowan branches. It's new moon tonight.'

New moon?! Ket felt the blood drain from his face. He'd been so busy and excited he hadn't noticed the passing of time. What if he was sent away tonight? He probably wouldn't even be here for the battle!

As he gathered branches in the forest, he felt as if he was preparing the coverings for his own burial shroud.

When he stumbled back to camp, Nessa flew towards him, her face shining.

'Did you see me?' she cried. 'Did you see me teaching Gortigern and Uncle Tirech, and all the others?'

Ket couldn't answer. He threw down his pile of branches and stared at them glumly.

'Hey, what's the matter?' Nessa tried to peer into his face.

'Tonight . . .' He raised his eyes. 'It's the new moon.'

To his amazement, a look of elation filled Nessa's face. She reached out to grip his hands. 'Don't worry.' The rod of her slingshot bit into his knuckles. 'You won't be sent away. I *know.* I promise.'

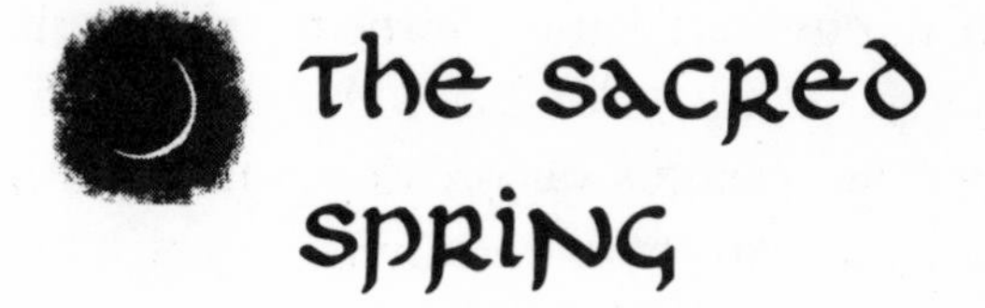

The Sacred Spring

Ket's feet almost danced around the fire as they called up the Spirit of the Moon.

'I'm staying, I'm staying!' The words sang in his head. He watched Nessa circling in front of him and wondered how she knew. He hurled his rowan branch at the flames with such enthusiasm, it soared over the top, and almost missed the fire, and when they settled down for the druid's announcement, he knew he was wearing a huge, foolish grin.

But when he turned to face the druid, he saw that Nessa, instead of taking her place with the fosterlings, was standing at Faelán's side, solemn-faced and rigid.

A jangle of alarm shot through him.

'Master Faelán,' said Nessa, 'I have something to say.' She sent Ket a brief, reassuring smile. 'I know that Ket . . . and Lorccán . . . still passionately want to be druids,' she went on. 'But, as for me . . .' She cleared her throat. 'I've changed my mind.' Ket's jaw dropped. 'I want to be apprenticed to Brehon Áengus. The law is supposed to be for everyone, from servant to chieftain, and I want to make sure that all the people in the tuath know their rights and privileges. Brehon Áengus doesn't . . . er . . .' She coloured, tugging one braid with her fingers, then went on in a rush. 'He doesn't have any assistants, and if I'm there to help him we can make sure that every person gets a fair hearing and a fair compensation. And then, one day, I will be the brehon!'

'So,' said Faelán, looking down at her, 'slowly, the stars are revealing their designs for all my fosterlings.'

No! No! Ket wanted to cry out the words, as he watched Nessa hand back her bells, but his mouth was too dry to make a sound.

'Nessa, you can't leave!' he wailed, a few minutes later, when Nessa was taking her last meal by the druid's fire. He leaned close to make himself heard above the racket. 'You always wanted to be a druid.

And . . .' He paused, gathering the courage to say something he'd never wanted to admit. 'And . . . and you're the best at everything.'

Nessa pried a limpet out of its shell and swallowed it before she raised her head.

'Ket, I always wanted to be a druid, but . . . there's not room for all of us, so now I've found something else to do. I'll be just as happy being a brehon. But you . . .' She looked at him earnestly. 'You only want to be a druid.'

'Yes, b—'

She pressed a finger over his lips. It smelt of fish. 'But you have to promise me to win,' she said. Her face was fiercely determined. 'Don't you dare let yourself get beaten by that gilded heap of conceit!'

She glanced at Lorccán.

Ket stared at her blazing green eyes, emotions whirling inside him. 'I'll win!' he vowed.

'And now . . .' Nessa stood up, brushing off her long skirt. 'It's time for me to go.'

'Nessa!' Ket scrambled to his feet and clasped her hands. They stared at each other, not speaking. Then Nessa turned her head and looked around the camp.

Ket followed, stumbling, as she crossed to the hollow oak and rested her hand on the trunk.

'Remember,' she said, and her voice was low and shaky, 'remember at Samhain, when we all hid in here together, and you were brave and went to the burial cairn?'

Ket nodded.

'Goodbye, tree,' whispered Nessa. Her eyes swept the clearing. 'Goodbye, fire. Goodbye, Sacred Yew.'

'Coming, Nessa?' Maura and Goll strode up and stood each side of her, like guards. 'Time to leave.'

Nessa brought her gaze back to Ket. Her eyes were brimming with tears. He stared at her, not trusting himself to speak.

'Goodbye, Ket,' she breathed. 'Goodbye.'

Next morning Ket prowled the camp on his own, head lowered, kicking at stones. He had not felt so lonely, so desolate, since his father had left him here more than five years before. His toe struck a wreath of ivy and he came to a halt. Slowly, he stooped to pick it up and a shower of faded celandine petals fluttered through his fingers. He stared. It was the head-dress Nessa had worn for Imbolc. The flowers were dead, but the leaves were still green.

Footsteps crunched behind him.

'So, it's you and me, Ket,' said a voice.

Ket's hands clenched convulsively as he rose and turned.

'Yes, Lorccán, it's you or me.'

Lorccán was wearing his usual confident smirk.

'Can you read that ogham message yet?' he demanded.

Ket glared at him, breathing hard. 'Can you?' he asked.

'Almost.'

But just at that moment Ket didn't care who could read the ogham. All he could think of was the expression on Nessa's face as she'd said her goodbyes.

With a clatter of their shields and swords, the warriors of the Ardal clan swept into camp. For once, Ket didn't turn to watch, but Lorccán scowled at them.

'It's not fair,' he muttered. 'I don't see why we can't have real swords too.'

Ket felt a slow grin spreading across his face.

'Nessa will have a sword,' he said. 'I bet she'll be fighting in the battle now.'

'Come on, you two,' called Goll, 'we're going to the Sacred Spring.'

'What for?' Ignoring each other, they galloped to join him.

'What are we going to do?' Ket's words tumbled out in excitement. This would be his first time at the Sacred Spring.

'Gortigern wants to make a sacrifice to ask for success in his battle,' said Goll.

Lorccán glanced, appalled, at all the shiny new weapons the men were carrying.

'Not those . . . they're not going to sacrifice those, are they?' he cried.

Goll shrugged.

'But that's such a waste!' Lorccán protested.

'It is never a waste to please a spirit.' Faelán's words rasped out reprovingly as he strode up behind them, the ornaments on his silver sandals tinkling. 'The Sacred Spring is the most powerful spirit of all. Water is both creator and destroyer of life.'

Lorccán looked abashed, and Ket felt a secret glee.

They made their way in single file along the river-bank, weaving among the willows and alders, with the river thundering over the rocks to their right. All around them the forest was wakening from the gloom of winter. The rain which had swollen the river had also washed the trees. The dark holly leaves were polished and gleaming, while green, hairy mosses draped wetly along the branches of the oaks. Song thrushes poured out their tunes, cawing rooks darted from tree to tree, and primroses, colt's-foot, snowdrops and starry blackthorn flowers lit up the undergrowth. Here and there, bare branches were breaking into leaf, and Ket caught a glimpse of a single fragile butterfly perching and fluttering among the trees.

The ground rose gradually steeper so that they bent forward, their breaths coming in quick pants.

Then suddenly the trees opened into a clearing and there was the spring, shadowed by an outcrop of rock, stretching at their feet. The noise of the rushing river and the calls of the birds faded away. Here was a stillness, and a waiting.

With barely a rustle of clothes or clink of weapons the warriors crept to the rim of the pool. They stared at the water that welled straight from the depths of the Underworld, from the home of the dead, from the world of the spirits. But all they could see in the still, black surface was the reflection of their own faces, their shining swords and their shields.

Faelán took Gortigern's sword and raised it in the air.

'Spirit of the Sacred Spring, accept these offerings and bring Gortigern victory and protection in his coming battle.'

He swung his arm. The sword flashed upwards, then sliced into the pool. It vanished instantly, but at the point where it entered the water, rings rippled outwards, silvery and shimmering, and merged together, like an orb floating on the blackness.

'A sign!' cried Faelán, pointing. 'The most auspicious day for your attack will be the next full moon.'

As the watching men broke into excited exclamations and began to hurl in more offerings,

Ket stared transfixed at the pin on Faelán's cloak. It was bronze, moulded in the shape of a stag. The last time he had seen that brooch, it was buried in the pit at Imbolc, sacrificed to Mother Earth.

'Look at that beautiful gold hilt! And that jewelled sheath. And that brand-new shield!' wailed Lorccán, as weapon after weapon tumbled into the pool.

'Don't you go getting ideas,' warned Goll. 'No sneaking back when everyone is gone. Anything that is given in sacrifice must remain forever where it lies.'

'I know,' groaned Lorccán.

'What about a druid?' asked Ket. 'Could he take a sacrifice out again?'

'Of course not,' said Goll. 'That would anger the spirits.'

Ket threw another bewildered glance at the pin on Faelán's cloak. 'It can't be the same brooch,' he thought. 'I must be mistaken.'

Everyone was leaving the spring now, tramping noisily around the edge and disappearing into the trees. In a few minutes, Ket was the only person left in the clearing. He stood, listening to the buzz of an insect, the *drip-drip* of water, and stared into the pool. There was no sign, no glimmer at all, of the treasures sunk in her depths. The spirit had accepted the offerings, and now she was silent again.

'And waiting,' mused Ket.

He felt as if the Sacred Spring was calling to him. Asking for one more sacrifice.

'But I don't have anything,' said Ket out loud.

He looked down at his clothes. He had no armbands, no silver ornaments on his laces, not even a buckle on his belt. And then he remembered the simple iron pin holding up his cloak. Slowly, he reached up and unclasped it. His cloak slithered to the ground and he stood there, the brooch clenched in his fist. He knew the iron would rust and dissolve in the water, but he had nothing else to offer. He raised his arm.

'Spirit of the Sacred Spring, accept this humble offering. Please help me win against Lorccán. Please, *please* let me be an anruth.'

There was a tiny splash, and the brooch was swallowed up in the blackness.

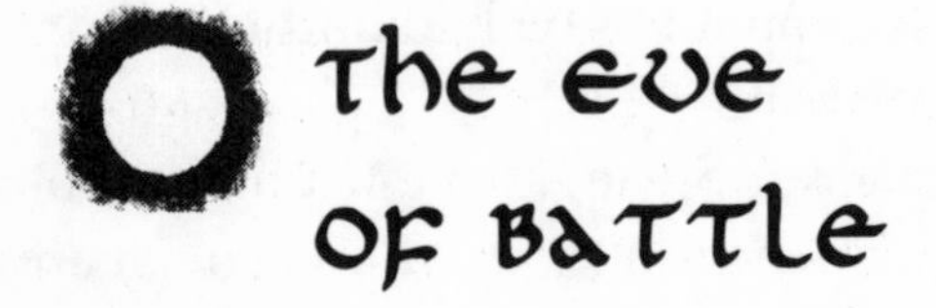

The Eve of Battle

It was the eve of the full moon. The Ardal clan was mustered for battle before the walls of Morgor. Up on the ramparts, Morgor's men watched with bows drawn.

On a flat stone in the centre of the Ardal camp lay the body of a sacrificed deer. Tirech and his brother lit a roaring fire nearby, and began to dig a cooking pit. Water seeped into the pit from the wet ground, and the two men rolled in hot stones from the fire. *Splash, splash, splash.*

Steam wafted from the pit.

'Druid, what are the portents?' called Gortigern.

The druid clumped towards the sacrifice on the makeshift altar, his cloak billowing and his long silver hair streaming backwards.

'I must re-e-ead the entrails.' His voice was quavering and hollow. It sounded like the voice of the wind.

He gazed at the bloody heap of innards spilled on the stone. There was silence except for the whisper of the wind and the crackle of the fire.

'Commence your attack at daybreak,' said the druid at last, 'from the direction of the rising sun. Morgor thinks he has nothing to fear from you. He will keep his main force within the ramparts.' Faelán's voice was scathing. 'He will leave his herdboys with their sticks and clods of earth protecting the cattle. He will send only his champion to challenge you in single combat.' The druid turned. His face glowed in the light of the fire and his tone rang with excitement and triumph. 'But you will annihilate these paltry defences! With the help of my magic arts, you will broach those high stone walls . . .'

The crowd exploded, shouting and thumping each other on the back. Ket had a glimpse of Nessa among the big burly men but when he tried to catch her eye, she vanished among the rabble. Tirech and his brother lifted the carcass of the deer and heaved it into the simmering water. Tirech's forehead gleamed with little beads of perspiration. A mead cup began to make its rounds. Gortigern broke into a loud, belligerent battle song, and the others joined in at the top of their voices, clapping and stamping in rhythm.

Ket felt a tug at his sleeve and turned to find Nessa by his side, her face flushed. He grabbed her by the arms as the crowd jostled around them, almost sweeping her away.

'Nessa! Are you all right?'

Nessa nodded vigorously. 'Brehon Áengus is teaching me the laws already. Did you know that girls are not supposed to inherit land or . . .' Ket could see the eagerness and enthusiasm in her eyes though her voice was drowned by the clamour of the crowd. She leaned towards him and he caught her final words. 'When I'm a brehon, I'm going to change all that!'

The wind rose in a sudden gust. Nessa's braids whipped across her cheeks, and the Ardal banner, with its white hound on a red ground, snapped and flapped on its pole.

There were worried shouts from behind, and Ket glanced over his shoulder. The anruth were grabbing at the pile of green rowan branches they had brought for the druid, catching them before they blew away. Art beckoned frantically at Ket.

'You'd better go,' said Nessa. She slid from his grasp and he had a last glimpse of gold beads dancing on the end of braids before she vanished into the mob.

'It is time to light the rowan fire,' Faelán declared. 'Ket, you may do the honours.'

Self-consciously, Ket drew a burning brand from the campfire. The wind almost blew it out, and he hastily bent double to protect it.

The anruth huddled close as he thrust the flame at the pile of green branches. He waited for long anxious moments with the wind whistling about his ears. At last, the rowan began to smoulder, and pungent smoke billowed outwards.

Faelán lifted his arms to mutter an incantation while Ket backed away, holding his hand over his nose and trying not to cough.

'O Rowan tree
O bringer of life and protection
Bring victory to the Ardal clan
Bring victory to Gortigern,'
chanted the druid.

Lorccán staggered through the smoke, carrying the cauldron, and lifted it onto the flames.

Soon, the fumes of healing herbs and burning rowan mingled with the smell of boiling deer flesh. Someone unsheathed his sword and began to sharpen it on a whetstone. The menacing *swish swish swish* sliced the air. The warriors crowded around the fire to paint their faces with soot and stiffen their hair with ashes and water. As Ket looked at the whitened locks twisted on their heads, and their eyes ringed in black, he felt his pulses quicken. In a few hours, they would be going into battle.

'Wish I could see Bran's face when they all come pouring through the gate,' said Lorccán.

'Bran?' Ket looked at Lorccán blankly, and then he remembered. Of course, Bran was one of Morgor's herdboys. He would be out there in the fields, trying to protect the cattle, when Gortigern struck.

'He'll be sorry he was always so nasty,' said Maura.

'Sorry?' chuckled Art. 'Bran doesn't know what sorry means.'

'He's going to be furious,' said Ket. 'He's cross enough being herdboy for a chieftain. Imagine what he'll think when Morgor becomes a commoner!'

'I don't think he'll be worrying overmuch,' said Goll, 'he'll most likely be dead.'

'Dead?!'

'It's a battle, remember, and if he's out there in the fields, well . . .' Goll shrugged. 'You heard what Faelán said, the defenders will be annihilated.'

Ket felt as if someone had poured icy water down his back.

'Yay!' crowed Lorccán. 'Then we can mash up his brains and turn him into brain balls!'

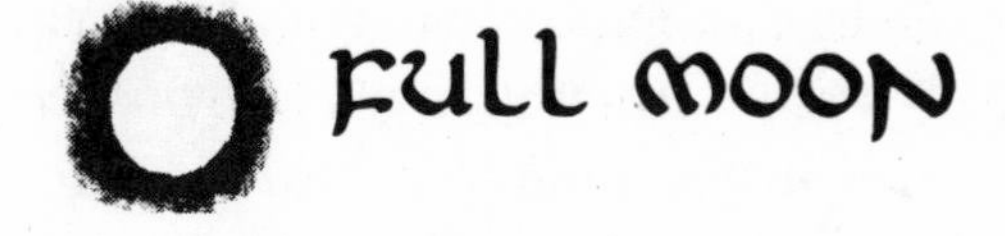

Full Moon

Alone before the fading embers of the fire, Ket gazed around the sleeping camp. By the full moon, he could make out the ghostly peaks of the tents where the men lay snoring, their feasting and drinking over. He could see the lookout guards nodding off, slumped against their halberds; and Faelán with his retinue, asleep in a huddle on the ground.

He peered beyond the black outline of a drystone fence into Morgor's fields. Was that dark patch a cluster of cows, or just bushes? Was that sound the shuffle of hoofs, or the pacing of a nervous boy? Was Bran sleepless too, staring back at the fires and the warriors, watching and afraid?

Ket rubbed his hands against his chest. He felt as if someone was squeezing it, making it hard to breathe. He'd never liked Bran. Nobody liked Bran. But still . . .

Ket closed his eyes and clenched his fists, trying to rekindle the fighting fever that had simmered inside him for the past month. He reminded himself that Morgor was the one who had stolen the lordship from his own father.

'Morgor deserves to be overthrown,' he growled.

But it wasn't true. In the years of Morgor's lordship there had been no discontent, no failure of crops, no terrible diseases, no burdensome taxes. And Morgor shared his wealth with generosity. They had all taken pride in the banquet he held for the king.

While as for Gortigern . . . Ket opened his eyes and scowled at the champion's tent, ringed by burning candles with big, bushy wicks.

'Just like the candles of a king,' he scoffed. 'He thinks he is such a grand, important personage.'

He thought of Tirech's struggle for compensation, he thought of Gortigern at the king's banquet striking his unarmed opponent with a dagger. Despite Nessa's words, despite the druid's declamations, Ket could not believe that Gortigern was worthy.

'He doesn't deserve to win. He doesn't deserve the druid's support. And Bran doesn't deserve to die!'

A picture of the deer's entrails, spattered and

bloody on the altar stone, rose in Ket's mind. He leapt to his feet, trying to escape the nauseating image, but now other pictures kept flashing into his head, imaginary pictures of Bran with dead unseeing eyes like the deer, Bran with his head chopped off, and his brains all . . .

Ket clutched his belly and vomited into the fire.

He sank down and buried his head in his hands.

'I can't let it happen,' he thought, 'I can't let it happen!'

There was a sourness in his mouth and it was not just from being sick. It was the taste of loss, of fear, of bewilderment. In his race to be the chosen anruth, he had thrown himself into every task that Faelán had set him, followed every command with blind faith. But this . . . he couldn't do it. Bran had been part of his life, part of his family. Ket couldn't stand by and let him be killed, just to glorify that bully Gortigern.

Ket stood up, his legs shaking. He would creep across to the fence, call out to Bran and warn him.

But even as the plan crossed his mind, he knew it wouldn't work. Even if Bran were awake, and heard him, he would scoff at Ket and refuse to believe, as he always had.

'Bran! Bran!' Ket groaned the name in frustration. 'What else can I do?' He gazed round helplessly at all the tents. So many of them! Every man and boy from the Ardal clan was there, and they'd even gathered supporters from other clans. 'There must be a hundred men here! If they attack, Bran doesn't stand a chance.'

Ket beat his fists despairingly against his thighs. What could he do? What could he *do*?

He longed to just turn and run, away from this terrifying threat, away from the battle. He wanted to run to the druid's camp, to the Sacred Yew and the hollow oak, back to a life that was familiar, and safe.

And suddenly, though he knew the clearing would be dark and deserted, he could resist no longer. Nobody stirred or called as he fled along the path, dodging between the tents. He stumbled into pools of mud, lurched out again and ran on. He reached the solid ground of the plain, his lungs struggling for air, and there, rearing in front of him, was the mound of the cairn, ghost-coloured in the moonlight.

He slowed, gasping for breath; and the next instant his mind was ablaze with a wild, impossible idea.

Ket threw himself at the boulder blocking the entrance to the tomb and, with all his desperate strength, heaved it out of the way. A wave of icy air, like the breath of death, poured over him. Ket recoiled, then, gathering his courage, he thrust himself into the narrow opening, slithering on the stones, and striking his head against the low ceiling.

His forehead throbbed as he stumbled forward, running his hands along the walls.

He reached the place where the tunnel opened into a chamber and straightened up, heart pattering wildly, ears filled with the rasp of his own frightened breathing. His eyes raked the darkness, seeking along the grey blur of stone walls for a glimmer of the silver horn.

It wasn't there.

His throat tightened as he took a tentative step, haunted by the memory of a dead white hand thudding onto his foot.

His toe clanged against something hard, and he stopped, frozen. Slowly, fearfully, he ran his gaze downwards. At his feet lay something faintly shiny. He let out a cry. Of course, the horn was lying on the floor, where he'd dropped it. He bent and scooped it up, but as he cradled it in his arms he saw that the silver no longer gleamed with newness. The long curve of metal was covered with holes and dints, the brightness tarnished.

Feverishly now, he plunged outwards, searching for the warriors. Dust billowed as he swept aside fragments of embroidered hangings. Rusty spears clattered to the stone floor. Bare bones rattled under his feet. For the first time, he noticed the grave goods arranged in the chamber – drinking horns studded with jewels, a wine flagon in a tarnished bronze stand, coloured beads in a circle with their thread rotted away.

But there was no sign of the Shadow Ones who had been here at Samhain. The warriors who might have protected Bran and led a charge against Gortigern were at last crumbled to dust. There was nothing left but their skeletons.

Ket sank to his knees.

'I destroyed them,' he said in an anguished moan.

For endless, agonising moments, Ket knelt there, the horn clutched in his arms, crushed with disappointment.

Then, as before, his hands, of their own volition, lifted the horn to his lips. This time, the sound when it came, was a plaintive note like the call of a plover.

The darkness around him stirred as if taking a breath. Dust clouds rose and swirled, though here under the ground there was no wind. The hard, gleaming whiteness of a bare skull wavered and softened. A luminous, transparent face hovered over it. For a moment, the bone still showed, then the flesh thickened and the skull faded. The next instant Ket was staring into a pair of dark, living eyes.

'Is it time?' asked a voice.

Ket couldn't speak. In front of him, the jumble

of bones and rusty metal had disappeared. In their place, the warriors with shining swords had returned. They were groaning and stretching as if waking from a sleep. One of them struggled upright, and Ket gaped at the dagger hilt protruding from his chest. Then, as they all began to stand, he saw that each bore the marks of battle, though none seemed disturbed by their ghastly injuries.

They were tall and bearded, clothed in rough fabrics and animal pelts. Over their long blond hair they wore strange bronze helmets decorated with animal horns, or even whole heads of wolves and eagles. Their shields were long, covering them from knee to brow, and made not of wood and iron, but of wicker or leather.

In a few minutes they were all standing. Watching him.

Ket rose, stumbling, to face them, and licked his dry lips.

'I . . . I have called you for battle,' he croaked.

They all nodded.

'We are the Tuatha de Danaan, and we will follow where'er you lead us, Master of the Horn,' said the first warrior. His voice was deep, resonating inside the stone chamber of the tomb.

Ket glanced down. The instrument in his grasp was now shining and new again. He cleared his throat.

'Uh . . . thanks. Well, er, let's go then.'

He turned to lead the way and felt the Shadow Ones close in behind him. His hands, gripping the horn, were sticky with sweat.

O Battle Lines

The cheerful *peep peep peep* of a robin broke the stillness. Ket tensed and lifted his head. He was so nervous he felt as if his body was on fire. Beside him, in the darkness, he was conscious of his band of warriors drawing themselves to attention.

There was a stirring in the battle camp in front of them, and as the dawn broke, the Ardal clan came charging up the slope, shields gleaming, spearheads glinting. 'Victory for Gortigern!' they yelled, in full-throated battle cry.

Then they skidded to a halt.

Standing in a row along the boundary of Morgor's fields, caught in the first beam of golden sunshine, were Ket and his band of warriors.

There was uproar from the clan of Ardal, and Gortigern pushed his way to the front, shaking his fist. He showed no sign of recognising Ket as he began to bawl, 'Who are you?! Morgor's nose-pickings? I am the champion of King Breasal! I am the one who brought Cellach o Muiredaich to his knees. I am the one who conquered Eochaid of the Seven Spears. Morgor is not even fit to wipe my backside! If you try to resist me, I will raze your walls and burn your homes and mash you into pulp!'

He paused to catch his breath and Ket flung back a retort.

'You can't! These warriors are the Tuatha de Danaan. You *can't* defeat them. They are dead already.'

Trembling, he held Gortigern's gaze. Around him, the men of the Ardal clan pressed close, muttering threats. Ket could almost feel their angry breaths.

All of a sudden, the mob parted, and Ket saw the druid moving through their midst, the smoke of the rowan fire wafting up behind him.

Ket felt a rush of guilt. Faelán's face was drained of colour and when he reached the front and pointed at Ket, his arm was trembling.

'What . . . is the meaning of this?' Faelán sounded old and bewildered.

Ket stood there, mute with agony. He wanted to protect Bran and defy Gortigern, but he hated to pit himself against his master. An agitated figure burst out of the crowd in front of him.

'Ket!' Nessa's face was distorted with shock. 'What are you *doing*?'

'I . . . I had to stop the battle,' Ket spoke at last, his voice quavering. 'So I fetched the Tuatha de Danaan.' He lifted his chin defiantly. 'Gortigern is not worthy to be chieftain.'

Nessa stared at him in disbelief.

'Druid!' Gortigern spat the word as he whirled round. 'Get rid of these . . . these . . .'

Faelán had not taken his eyes from Ket. Now, slowly, very slowly, he lowered his arm and shook his head.

'I am afraid that is not possible.' His voice sounded hollow and distant. 'My magic arts will be of no avail against the Shadow Ones.'

He turned, tottering slightly, so that the anruth rushed to support him, and the crowd parted to let them through. Lorccán cast a triumphant glance in Ket's direction before he followed in their wake.

'But . . . wait . . .' Gortigern sputtered.

In a fury of spite, the champion spun round and hurled his spear at the Tuatha de Danaan. Ket dived out of the way but it thudded into the man beside him. As the Ardal clan let out a roar, the Tuatha de Danaan warrior glanced down, tugged the spear from his chest and dropped it disdainfully on the ground.

Taking a breath, Ket raised the horn and blew a short, rousing blast.

As one man, the Shadow Ones lifted their swords. With one voice, they let out a bellow.

The Ardal clan turned and fled, Gortigern in the lead.

Ket lowered the horn and stared at their retreating backs. In a moment the battleground was deserted. The Tuatha de Danaan were once more silent and motionless.

'Well, well,' mocked a familiar voice behind him. 'Aren't you the big hero?' It was Bran, standing by the fence, hands on hips and a derisive expression on his face. 'I suppose you expect us to fall down and kiss your feet?'

'I . . .' Ket felt his cheeks flush. 'It doesn't matter what you think,' he muttered.

Bran raised his eyebrows.

'Well, and what are you going to do now? I don't reckon Old Feather-cloak is exactly going to welcome you back with open arms.'

Ket couldn't reply. He had been carried away on a wave of bravery and defiance. But now . . . Faelán and the anruth would despise him. By his one desperate act he had made himself an outcast. He could never return to the druid's camp. That last image of Lorccán's face, lit by an exultant gleam, rose to taunt him. He turned his back on Bran.

'Come on,' he mumbled to the Tuatha de Danaan. 'I'll take you home.'

They followed, silent as they had come. No footfalls, no clatter of weapons. They flowed back into the tomb. When he came to a halt in the dark chamber he could feel them clustered around him, waiting and watching.

'Thank you,' he whispered. He peered into the gloom, trying to see the faces of these men who had risen from the past and obeyed his command, but all he could distinguish was shadowy outlines and the glimmer of helmets. 'Thank you,' he repeated. 'You may rest again now.'

He bent and laid the horn on the ground. It clinked as it touched the cold stone. He waited a moment, his head bowed. When he raised his eyes, the warriors had sunk to the floor, and already he could see the white of their bones. Without looking back, he groped his way to the door.

Ket was so still, sitting with his back against an oak tree, that the squirrel paid him no attention. She scuttled down the trunk, used his shoulder to launch herself to the ground, then picked up an acorn in her front paws and began to nibble. Her coat was brown with a russet tinge along her back and tail, and as she moved, the sun seemed to tip every hair with gold.

'Like Nessa's hair,' thought Ket.

As the squirrel twitched her head from side to side, eyes constantly shifting, ears twisting, he felt his own senses sharpen. Slowly he became aware of the sounds she was listening to: the rain trickling through the branches, the busy chirrup of birds, the rustle of beaks prodding for insects. He smelled the damp earth and imagined he could taste the nut she was nibbling. When she turned it in her paws, he felt it was his own hands moving.

Then suddenly a wave of anger swept through him, and he sprang to his feet.

'I don't *need* to watch you any more,' he yelled. As the startled squirrel bounded for cover, he shouted after her. 'There's no point now! I'm never going to be a druid!'

Ket swayed, dizzy with hunger and weariness.

For three days he'd been running away. Running from Morgor's high stone walls, from Lorccán's smirk and Nessa's bewilderment, running from the fury of the Ardal clan, the champion Gortigern, and the memory of the hurt reproach in Faelán's eyes.

'But I had to do it, I *had* to!' Ket cried out loud.

His words, swallowed up by the trees, sounded futile and pathetic. The animals were silent now, as if shocked by his betrayal. The air filled with the scent of wet leaves and the *splish splosh* of rain. Ket began to shiver in his clammy clothes. He wrapped his arms around himself and squatted down, his teeth chattering.

His virtuous defiance was trickling away. In its place, a misery of shame was creeping over him. Who was he, a mere fosterling, to have questioned the wisdom of the druid? Faelán knew everything in the world, and could foretell the future. If Faelán had seen a vision that Gortigern should be chieftain, then it must be true.

'But,' queried a small, insidious voice in his head, 'did Faelán really have that vision?'

Ket tried to push the doubt away. His master was a man of honour; he would never lie about a vision, he would never abuse the trust that people placed in him.

Or would he?

All of a sudden, images, searing and hideous as vomit, poured into Ket's mind: the druid crawling into his hut to escape the wind and rain, the druid counting his gifts of gold from Gortigern, the druid clumping around in silver sandals, the druid wearing a bronze brooch stolen from the sacrifice . . .

Questions and doubts whirled in Ket's head. Had Faelán become so puffed up with his own importance that he no longer respected the spirits, no longer respected his own teachings? Or . . .

A worse thought struck Ket. It was like a physical blow, making him cry out.

Maybe the teachings were a lie! Maybe the rituals were a sham. Maybe . . . maybe Bran was right. Ket buried his face in his hands. For five years and more he had yearned to be a druid; he had worshipped Faelán with blind, unswerving faith. But now . . . if druids were ordinary people, if none of their teachings were true, then he had wasted all those years of his life. He had nothing. *Nothing!* Desperately, he tried to conjure up a fury of indignation, but all he could feel was loss. He felt as if someone had torn out his heart and left a great, gaping hole.

He sat, unable to move, while the dank and dark of evening wrapped around him.

With the first light of dawn, the squirrel poked her head up from her drey. She gave herself a vigorous scratch, and glanced round with bright, inquisitive eyes. Ket still huddled motionless at the foot of the tree. Keeping a wary eye on him, she ventured down the trunk to her secret hoard of nuts.

Ket was hollow with hunger. The sight of the squirrel nibbling broke through his fog of misery. He swayed forward.

'Please, Squirrel, may I have some of your acorns?'

The squirrel hardly paid attention as he inched towards her, eased his hand into the hollow and drew out a few nuts.

'Thank you,' he breathed.

The damp had caused the acorns to sprout, and leached out some of their bitterness. Ket and the squirrel chewed together in companionable silence. Ket felt a tiny flicker of pride. A few weeks ago, the squirrel would have fled if he'd tried to come so close. It was only by watching, as Faelán had instructed, that . . .

Ket stopped in mid bite.

'It's all true!' he squawked, struggling to keep his voice soft so he wouldn't frighten the squirrel. He felt light-headed with relief. Faelán had strayed from his own teachings, but that didn't mean those teachings were false. 'No ordinary person could have taught me how to make friends with a squirrel!'

Suddenly he could see the druid again in the full glory of his power: sweeping away the wind with a branch of broom, casting Ossian down with a pointed finger, and passing across the earth with footsteps as light as the tread of a butterfly.

Ket was elated, his agony of doubt swept away. He straightened up and looked at his surroundings for the first time.

Spring had clearly arrived in this little wood. The willows and ash trees were green with new, young leaf, and there were bluebells and primroses everywhere. He scrambled to his feet and began to pluck primrose heads, stuffing the yellow petals ravenously into his mouth. Led by the sound of running water, he pushed through a thicket of alder trees, and fell to his knees on the bank of a brook. He scooped water in his hands and gulped thirstily.

The stones of the river were encrusted with long

black mussels. Seizing a sharp rock, Ket hacked one free, then glared at the tightly closed shell in frustration. With no fire for cooking, how was he supposed to open it? He slammed it against the rocks, and attacked it with his sharp stone. Finally, with bruised fingers, he pried it open, scraped out the yellow, rubbery flesh, then closed his eyes and let it slide down his throat.

'Thank you, Spirit of the River,' he murmured, 'thank you for this sustenance.'

His eyes flew open again and he reached forward to attack another mussel. The sun rose above the tree tops, the birds twittered, an early dragonfly hummed across the water, and the scent of primroses wafted from the warming earth.

At last, Ket rocked back on his heels. He could not endure the taste of one more raw mussel. He gazed down at his hands, seeing, not the empty shell in his fingers, but the druid's camp. He was imagining the warmth of the campfire, with Goll, Art, Bronal and Maura gathered around. He was smelling the scents of hare stew boiling in the cauldron, and burning rowan branches. He was watching the druid gaze up at the sky, reading the omens in the clouds.

Ket heaved a deep, regretful sigh. Never again would he be part of that scene. Never again would he have the right to carry a branch of bells. And never, now, would he learn how to read the omens. He would live with Ragallach, just as his family had always planned. He would grow up to be an ordinary man, with no knowledge of spells, or the making of wands, or the art of healing. Just an ordinary farmer going on raids, ploughing fields, mucking out pigsties.

Mournfully, he tossed aside the mussel shell and rose to his feet. It was time to go.

There was a path of broken branches where he had battered his way through the alder thicket. When he emerged on the other side, he cast around for other signs that would show him the way he had come. Slowly, he began to pick his way along an elusive trail of snapped twigs and trampled grass, back through the unfamiliar woodland.

'At least, with all that training to notice things around me, I'll never get lost!' he mused.

Somehow, the thought seemed to make him more miserable.

For four days he tramped, sustaining himself with raw buds and leaves, and sucking the sweet spring sap from birch twigs. This time he moved stealthily, hiding if he heard voices, for only a druid could venture beyond the borders of his tuath without fear of attack.

At night he lay alone on the ground, staring up at the stars, wondering what future they foretold for him.

On the fifth morning, as he lay listening to the

dawn chorus, still half-asleep, he was startled by a crashing through the undergrowth. In a flash, he was scrambling up the trunk of a yew tree to hide in its branches. He waited for a stag to come flying through the trees pursued by hunters, but instead, it was a bunch of fians who sprang into view, galloping and hallooing on their horses. To Ket's dismay, they drew rein beneath him. They were young, lithe and brown as fawns, their hair matted with mud and leaves, and so close he could smell the sweat from their unwashed bodies. He stared in alarm at their beasts, snorting, stamping and swishing their tails at the foot of his tree, muscles rippling in their huge rumps.

The fians were holding nets in their hands, with stones tied to the corners. They laughed and pointed at the birds darting around in alarm. Then they slid off their horses' backs and sprang up into the trees, whirling their nets in the air, and trapping the fluttering creatures.

Terrified, Ket cowered in his hiding place, almost suffocated by the acrid smell of the yew needles. He saw one fian find a blackbird's nest, toss the three tiny eggs into his mouth, and crunch them up, shell and all.

When they had a pile of thrushes, pigeons and blackbirds lying dead with their necks wrung, the fians began to tear the living branches off the trees to make a campfire. They kindled a flame with flint and steel, and skewered the birds on stripped hazel sticks. Ket's mouth watered as the smell of broiling bird flesh reached his nostrils.

'Hey, look at that strange bird, there!' yelled a voice, and Ket's heart stopped beating as a dirty hand pointed up at him.

Ket flung himself out of the yew, landing on all fours, but as he leapt to his feet to flee, a net crashed over his head and shoulders, and jerked him backwards.

'What shall I do with this one?' asked his captor, hauling Ket over to the fire.

'Not much of a catch. Doesn't look like he has any gold.'

'Might have a bit of meat on him though.'

The boy pinched Ket's arm.

Ket kicked out, wriggling desperately. They all laughed in derision.

'Ach, stop your teasing. Leave him be. He's no use to us.' The last speaker was the only one old enough to grow a beard. He stretched, scratched his belly, and stood up. 'Come on, let's be on our way.'

A moment later, the horses had pushed through the bushes and vanished, and Ket was left alone, staring at a few quivering leaves.

Falling on his knees, he rummaged hopefully among the powdery ashes of the fire, but there was not an ember left, nor a morsel of meat. The fians had picked every bone clean. He flopped back, almost weeping in disappointment.

Later that day, as dusk was falling, Ket reached the walls of Morgor's fort. Emotions of pride, defiance and regret all surged inside him. This was the place where he had defeated his master.

From here, he could cut through the forest and reach his old ringfort before it grew dark. Or . . . He hesitated, staring across the marsh. He could take the route through the bog and up onto the plain. He could feast his eyes on the druid's camp one last time, before he started his new life.

Ket waited for the cover of night. It was the dark half of the month and the moon would not rise for several hours. Moving as quietly and gently as a mist, he crossed the Plain of Moytura. He circled the cairn, no longer afraid of the dead within, and slipped into the forest. Creeping to the edge of the trees, he peeped through the branches.

The camp was spread before him. He could see the sprawling outline of the Sacred Yew with the pale shape of the ogham rod at its roots. He could see the campfire, and everyone gathered around it. Faelán had his back to Ket, telling a tale and the others were listening, faces golden in the firelight.

Ket craned forward, aching with yearning. He wanted to be with them, part of that circle. But he couldn't even hear Faelán's words. He was an outsider now. Just an onlooker.

The druid threw his arm around the figure beside him, and the boy turned. It was Lorccán. Ket clutched the tree beside him, shaken by a wave of anger and envy.

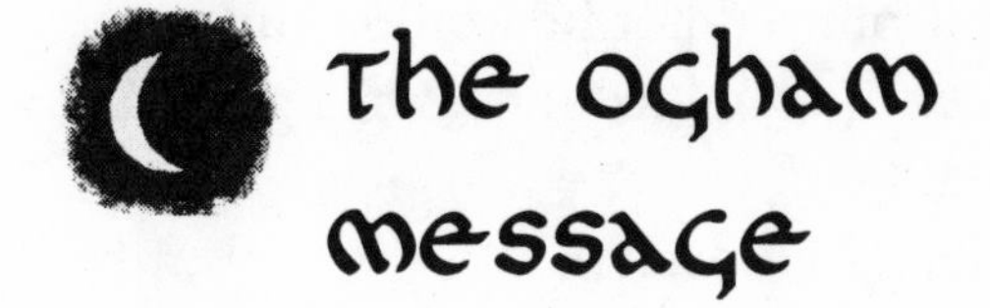

The Ogham Message

Ket lay in the darkness, eyes closed, but he couldn't sleep. Images kept tumbling through his mind: Faelán in his feather cloak, Lorccán grinning, the battle encampment, the walls of Morgor's fort . . . He shot upright, feeling that every hair on his body was standing on end.

Morgor's fort! He saw it again as it had looked this evening. Only now, the quiet and peace of the scene struck him as sinister. Why had there been no sounds or movements? Why had he seen no archers on the ramparts? A dreadful realisation crept over him. Of course, as soon as he and the Shadow Ones had left, Gortigern's men had returned! With the aid of the druid they had defeated Morgor. And . . .

Ket's heart turned over.

And slaughtered Bran.

Ket let out a groan of despair. He had made himself an outcast, and allowed Lorccán to win, all for nothing! And then another thought stabbed him. He guessed that Nessa had given up her place, left to be a brehon, just so he would have the chance to win. He had promised her he would. And now . . . He threw himself on the ground, curling up like a wounded animal.

He must have fallen asleep, for when the dawn chorus began, he was dreaming of learning his first feda. He lay with his eyes shut, clinging to the warm memory of Goll inclined towards him, smiling and friendly, but, too soon, the last wisps of the dream faded.

He shivered, and sat up, hugging himself and rubbing his arms. The dew had been falling, and his clothes were damp and cold. He blinked around, trying to get his bearings. Last night, he had blundered around in the darkness, eyes blurred with tears. Now, the sun shone blindingly through the trees, and drops of water sparkled on twigs and tender young leaves. Ket ran his eye down the smooth, greenish trunk beside him, and stopped with a gasp.

There, scraped into the bark, were familiar signs. This was the ash tree where Goll had taught him his first feda!

Immediately, it seemed that the figure from his dream was seated beside him again. Ket could see the hand reaching out and cutting the marks into the tree. Goll had started from the bottom, and then . . .

Ket let out a cry.

Goll had started from the *bottom*!

Ket clapped his hand over his mouth and stared at the feda with wide, shocked eyes. When he had tried to read ogham himself, he had worked from the top down. That meant he had read Cormac's name upside-down! That meant the sounds he had worked out were all wrong. The *o* must be *a*, the *r* must be *m*. And, of course, every time he'd tried to read the ogham rod, that had been the wrong way too!

He pressed his palms against his eyes. The message was burned into his memory, just as Faelán had scorched it in the birchwood. He opened his eyes again, feverishly cleared a patch on the ground, and scraped the message in the earth.

There was one feda carved at the bottom, five straight lines with a stem going up the middle. That must be the first word. He clenched his fists in frustration. It was a feda he didn't know!

He glared at the ash tree, urging it to speak, and saw his own wobbly effort at drawing *nuin*. Suddenly, he heard Goll's voice.

'Don't forget to put the stemline in. On the left. Otherwise it could be *quert* or *iodo*.'

Ket's heart seemed to stop beating as he stared at the five straight lines. With a stemline up the middle, it had to be *quert* or *iodo*.

'Of course!' cried Ket out loud. 'It's *iodo*! The first word is *I*!'

And the second word? Those two feda were both in Cormac's name. That word was easy now. And the last word? Of *course*, it didn't start with *h-t*. It *ended* with *t-h*! That made sense.

He sank back on his heels, shaking all over.

There was one feda that he didn't know. But he didn't need to know. Suddenly he could read the whole word. The whole message.

'But it's not true!' he whispered. 'I can read the message, but it's not true!'

'Ket!'

Ket swung round in shock. It was Faelán. The druid had glided up as silent as of old for he was not wearing his silver sandals. He looked frail and elderly, his hair and beard turned pure white.

'Master!' squeaked Ket, and stumbled to his feet.

'You have returned,' said Faelán.

'I . . .' Ket stared at Faelán in bewilderment. There was no anger in the druid's expression, no accusation. He seemed – almost – to be pleading.

Ket gulped.

'Will you *let* me come back?' he asked in a rush.

The druid held out his arms.

Ket flung himself forward. For the first time in his life, he was wrapped in the druid's arms. They felt thin and brittle as dry twigs. 'I was afraid we'd lost you,' murmured Faelán.

Ket brushed the back of his hand across his eyes. He was laughing and crying at the same time.

'But hasn't Lorccán become your next anruth?' he asked.

The druid shook his head. 'It has not yet been the next new moon.'

'And . . . and Gortigern,' asked Ket urgently, 'what has happened with Gortigern?'

'Ah.' Faelán stroked his beard. 'He wanted to attack again, but I told him the portents were against him.' The corners of his eyes crinkled, and then he astounded Ket by winking.

Ket stared, and suddenly he understood. A true druid could read the portents and foretell the future, but sometimes . . .

'Now . . .' Faelán's expression changed and he took Ket's arm. 'Come and look.' His fingers felt like a bird's claw.

They stepped from the trees and the druid pointed dramatically at the camp. In the daylight, Ket could see that the stone hut was gone.

'And all the gold, and the silver sandals,' said the druid earnestly. 'I cast them in the Sacred Spring. And I implored the spirits to send you back.'

His pale, transparent eyes gazed into the distance. 'I taught you fosterlings the principles of druidry.

I preached to you about learning the natural order, about valuing every life, about sharing, and being honourable. But I was so carried away by my own loftiness . . .' He drew in his breath and straightened his shoulders. 'I began to treat those rules with contempt.' His eyes came back to Ket. Tiny white clouds floated in their blueness. 'When you had to defy me in order to obey my own teachings, you revealed to me how far I had gone astray.'

Ket felt his cheeks grow hot, but before he could reply, there were shouts all around the camp.

'Ket!' 'It's Ket!' 'He's back!'

In a moment they were thundering towards him. Bronal hooted, Art thumped his shoulder and Goll ruffled his hair. Maura bounced up and down, her cheeks pink, her straw-coloured locks wilder than ever.

Behind their excited faces, Ket spied Lorccán. The gazes of the fosterlings locked. Lorccán's eyes blazed a challenge, and then, slowly and belligerently, he crossed his arms.

It was six days until the next new moon.

The Fifth Moon

While Ket had been gone, Lorccán had wormed his way into the everyday life of the anruth. He had taken over Art and Bronal's role of tending the fire. All through the day, he ostentatiously dragged long, heavy branches into camp, which he broke up noisily to add to his wood heap. When Ket tried to put a log on the flames, Lorccán elbowed him out of the way, telling him it was the wrong type of wood.

'Faelán wants to burn juniper today,' he said bossily.

He slid his eyes round to see how Ket reacted. Ket kept his expression blank.

Lorccán had appointed himself Maura's helper.

That night, instead of everyone crowding around the cauldron after Faelán was served, Lorccán solemnly handed out portions like the rannaire at a king's banquet. After he served himself, he sat down to eat, pretending to forget about Ket. He looked annoyed when Ket rose, and without comment scraped the last dregs from the pot.

'If you want to get close to the Greater Harmony you really have to feel the ground, you know,' instructed Lorccán next morning as Ket was tying his brogues.

Ket looked up in surprise and saw that Lorccán was now barefoot like the anruth and Faelán. Ket pursed his lips and dragged off his shoes again.

'Your feet won't be tough like mine, though,' said Lorccán. 'Look.' He snatched a holly branch from his wood pile and stamped on the prickly leaves. 'See? Bet you can't do that.'

He threw out the challenge, and stood back, waiting for Ket to copy.

'No, I can't do that yet,' Ket replied. And he smiled calmly into Lorccán's astonished face. For Ket was hugging a secret to his heart, a secret that warmed him like fire.

'Lorccán, you can have your last few moments of glory,' he thought. 'You'll be gone soon. *I'm* the one who can read the ogham.'

It seemed no time at all till the sun was setting on the evening of the new moon.

Ket picked up his branch of bells, noticing how dull the bronze had become.

'It's the last night you'll be needing those!' said Lorccán smugly.

'Yes,' said Ket. 'Tomorrow,' he thought, 'tomorrow I'll have a branch of silver bells.' Every nerve in his body was twanging with excitement.

Lorccán had heaped the fire high, and as he handed out the rowan branches he wore a broad grin.

'Your last time!' he said to Ket.

Ket barely heard him.

Moving sunwise, the druid started around the fire. Lorccán pranced at his heels and the others fell in behind. Ket brought up the rear. When Faelán completed his circle and came to a halt, Lorccán was on his right side, and Ket on his left.

The druid raised his arm.

'Spirit of the Moon
Arise from darkness.
Spirit of the Moon
Return and guide us.'

Slowly, slowly, the sunset faded, and there, where the druid pointed, the new moon was rising.

There was a hush. All eyes turned to the druid.

'The final reckoning is here,' said Faelán. 'Only two fosterlings remain.' Majestically, he turned to the Sacred Yew. The birch rod, held fast by the roots of the tree, glowed in the firelight. 'Five moons ago, I inscribed that message in ogham.' They all stared, intent and expectant. 'I gave you warning,' Faelán intoned, 'that only the one true anruth would succeed in reading its secret.'

Ket began to quiver with excitement.

Without a sound, the druid skimmed across the ground, stooped down and released the rod from the sacred tree's keeping. He turned and held it outwards. 'Lorccán!' he demanded. 'Can you read this message?'

Ket felt exultation bubbling up inside him. He was going to burst, like a seedpod exploding in the sun.

Lorccán accepted the rod and held it before his eyes.

'I—,' he began in a loud confident voice.

There was a screaming sound in Ket's head and he couldn't breathe.

Then the golden boy faltered. He scowled and bit his lip. 'Do? Be?' He glanced up inquiringly as if he expected Faelán to prompt him, but the druid stood with his hand resting on the tree, his face expressionless.

Lorccán swung round on Ket, the rod clenched in his fist as if it was a dagger. 'Anyway, I bet *you* can't read it!'

Faelán raised one eyebrow. 'Ket?'

Ket's whole body was suddenly glowing as if he was

on fire. When he took the rod, his hands shook, and the sooty black marks swam in front of his eyes.

'Yes, I can read it,' he whispered.

'Ha, I don't believe you.' Lorccán crossed his arms.

Ket glanced down. His hands had stopped shaking. He could see the first word *I* and the second word *am.* He drank in the last, precious word and drew a deep breath. He lifted his gaze.

They were all watching him: Lorccán, tense and apprehensive now, Goll beaming, Maura nodding encouragement, Art and Bronal breathless and eager. Just for a moment, the faces of those who had been sent away seemed to float there too: Riona, Bran, Nath-í and Nessa. For one heart-wrenching instant, Ket felt a pang of loss. Then the glow of victory poured over him. The others were gone, and he was the winner.

Thrilling with happiness and pride, he raised the rod aloft, and spoke out loud the secret words: 'I . . . am . . . anruth!'

Faelán nodded and his mouth quirked in a smile.

'Yes!' shouted Maura, clapping her hands.

'He did it, he did it!' Art and Bronal jigged up and down in excitement.

Goll applauded, laughing.

Only Lorccán stood still, his face drained of colour.

'I'm sorry, Lorccán,' murmured Ket.

Lorccán flung up his head. 'I don't need your pity!' But in the firelight Ket could see that his eyes glistened with tears.

There was a peal of golden bells and everyone turned. Faelán laid a hand on Ket's shoulder.

'Ket, the ogham rod has led us to you. It has chosen someone of power and strength.' He looked around the circle of intent, watching faces. 'When Ket was merely a lad at his mother's knee, he resisted the magic words I used to foment his father's downfall. He cannot be influenced by the enchantment of my harp. He bends the Shadow Ones to his will. He has even . . .' the druid's face crinkled in a smile 'withstood my own persuasive powers. Above all . . .' His voice grew solemn. Ket tried to swallow but his throat was rigid. 'Above all, Ket is keen, observant and thoughtful of others. Ket is a true anruth.'

The white bones were still scattered on the floor. The silver horn lay beside them, tarnished once more, and covered with dust. Ket raised the candle higher. Soft, wavering light played over the shredded hangings on the walls, and jewels winked at him out of the gloom.

Ket could see the three chambers Faelán had described, opening off the main tomb. They were small and shadowy, too low to stand in. Ket moved towards them, treading so carefully in his bare feet that even the dust was not disturbed. On the floor of the first chamber he could see the huge stone dish carved with strange swirls. One day, he would learn the meaning of those swirls, but now his task was to place the honey cake on the dish.

As he leant forward, hot candle-fat dripped on his fingers. He let out a yelp and dropped the candle. The flame snuffed out and blackness wrapped around him. He stood a moment, sucking his burnt fingers, then eased closer till his shins pressed against the stone. Stooping he set down the cake, still warm and sticky from the fire. It was a gift for the Shadow Ones.

He paused, listening, but there was no sound bar the *thud thudding* of his own heart. Only a short time since, he would have been too terrified to spend a night in a grave with the dead, but now he knew the Shadow Ones would not harm him.

Groping on the floor beside the stone, as Faelán had instructed, his fingers closed on something small and hard. His breath caught. It was a branch of bells. The new branch with the silver bells. The branch of an anruth.

As he lifted it in his hand, it sent out a musical tinkle, and he felt a shock of pride. The sound was different from the bronze bells he'd carried before. Growing accustomed to the gloom now, he could see the shimmer of their silver. He turned his eyes and made out the faint, curving shapes of the walls. Slowly, carefully, he worked his way to the next chamber. It was so small, he had to crawl inside, the skirt of his new, long robe tangling around his legs. He wriggled around to face the way he'd come, propped his back against the stone wall and peered into the darkness.

This vigil in the tomb was the final step in his initiation. When the anruth had woken him before the dawn, they'd been carrying burning branches of juniper. They had chanted and circled around him till the air was saturated with aromatic, purifying fumes. They had cut off his long, tangled locks, taken away his old clothes, and cast them into the fire. With his eyes smarting from the smoke, Ket had watched his old life smoulder away.

The anruth had lifted him then, bearing him on their shoulders to the Sacred Spring. Ket had bathed in the icy waters, clinging tight to Goll's hand so he would not be sucked down into the Underworld. And finally, he had dressed in the grey robe that Maura had dyed for him with bearberry leaves.

Ket closed his eyes now, remembering his reflection in the Sacred Spring – just like all the other anruth, with a long grey robe, and a silver fillet bound round his hair. He imagined how Nessa would shriek with excitement when she saw him come strutting up in his new garb. He was not sure he could believe it himself! Only a few hours ago, he'd still been wearing his old léine and trews. He grinned, and opened his eyes.

A speck of gold was glinting in the darkness. He jerked upright. The next moment, the first ray of the rising sun shone through the entrance of the tomb, a single finger of light stretching across the floor. It reached to the walls curving around him, and then poured over his knees, bathing him with sunlight.

The long wait was over. Ket's first day as an anruth had begun.

In the world of Viking Magic
a mark scratched in stone can take away pain
a cloak can save you from drowning
a boy can turn into a lynx

But what if the magic is back-to-front?

Runestone, and its companion novels, *Wolfspell* and *Stormriders*, are stories of magic, mystery and excitement set in the world of the Vikings.